THE
FIRST
STROKE

THE
FIRST
STROKE

by

Cappy Kotz
(aka)
Crystal Bailey

Lace Publications

Lady Winston Series

Library of Congress Cataloging-in-Publication Data
Kotz, Cappy, 1955-
   The first stroke.

   (Lady Winston series)
   1. Lesbianism—Fiction.   2. Erotic stories, American.
I. Title.   II. Series.
PS3561.0848F57 1988   813'.54   88-13289
ISBN 0-917597-13-3

Printed in the United States of America.
First Edition.   First printing.

Cover photo of the author by Jacquie (J.C.) Collins
Cover design by Lambda Graphics, Denver

Lace Publications
POB 10037
Denver CO 80210-0037

ISBN 0-917597-13-3

In honor of, and with thanks to the many who've inspired and given their support, namely:

Mitar and Alice, Phrin, Dennise, Karen, Lamar, Beth and Anne, Miss OakGrove Herself, and my community.

TABLES OF CONTENS

Take Me Down

Make Me Listen

Let Me Go, Cum Forever On My Lips

Take Me Down

Click

The night was dark and warm. My inner thighs and cunt, awakened by the motorcycle between my legs, tingled with honest heat as I parked the bike and crossed the street to the bar. It was smoky inside, loud, and packed with women. I had passed several groups of them taking a break outside. They watched me walk by, in my black boots and black leather jacket, three slitted bandanas around my neck, and a fourth one sticking up out of my back pocket. I had my right hand in a front pocket, so's to cup myself, all the while thinking about pressing one of the women on that dark, dirty street into the shadows, and making her go down on me.

I leaned on the bartop with elbows and forearms, hooked my boot heel over the rail near the floor, and ordered a beer, angling my legs slightly apart so the crotch seam of my jeans pulled tight. It was too hot for my jacket. I took it off, pushed through the crowd and asked the bouncer if I could stash it behind the door. She was big and round, molded by her clothes, and smelled of patchouli. I had to press my mouth close to her ear so she could hear what I was saying over the throb of the music, and in doing so, grazed her substantial bosom with my shoulder. When she made room for me to get behind her and toss my jacket down, I purposely slid my cunt along the fabric covering her backside.

Back at the bar, I drank my beer and ordered another, fingering the bandanas around my neck. Two of them were black, one cobalt blue; I'd cut and hemmed the slits in them myself. Across the room, Tammy caught my eye. Her butt was the best part about her, nice and big. She was dressed, as usual, in a short skirt. I used to take her shopping just so I could watch her put them on and take 'em off. I went right into the dressing room with her and stayed in the corner on a chair, though I wanted to fuck her up against the mirror.

Across the bar room, Tammy smiled at me. I tipped my beer and finished it; dug some change out of my pocket to leave as a tip, and glanced sidelong at Tammy to see if she'd noticed me furtively groping my cunt at the same time. She did. I felt her eyes, over the shoulder of her lover, trying to unzip me. I walked away, willing her to remember how it used to be, the muscles of my ass clenching beneath the urgent plea of her hands shoving me deeper.

The dance floor was wild with girls. The room smelled of cunt, and there were far too many zippers and buttons keeping it all under wraps. I slouched against the wall in my white short sleeve shirt with the sleeves rolled up so as to show my arms. I'd worked my punching bag over earlier and felt pumped; thick and powerful across my chest and in the arms, long and lean in the hips and upper legs. My boots were the fancy kind with stitching up the sides, cowboy style.

"Hey, K.C.!"

I looked to my left and saw Cheryl, slim buddy of mine, waving at me over the heads of dancing women. She wore a blue alligator shirt, jeans, high top tennies, had let her blonde hair get a little long, almost to her collar. I approved of the change. It softened her face.

"How're you doing?!" she yelled after making her way through the packed swaying room to my side. She wedged in close. I noticed that one of the buttons securing her fly was undone. "What have you been up to?" she asked, her breath hot along the rim of my ear.

"Looking!"

She arched both eyebrows in utter, lustful agreement.

The music came up through the floorboards and mixed with the pulse in my loins. It got up under my ribs, and made me snap my fingers to its beat. Cheryl looked as if she might hump anyone who'd let her. Her shirt sleeve sanded my skin with its clean texture as she craned her neck and ogled first one woman then another. Her lively motion brought her healthy sweat smell to my nostrils.

"My God!" Cheryl's body went live-wire tight as she made an all out effort not to gape at a woman whose electric blue leotard barely covered her pert breasts. The woman turned and insinuated her arms around her partner's neck; they danced slow, unsheathed, practically fucking on the floor. The partner wore black levis and a shirt of the same color. Her hair was greased back.

Someone howled energetically as an uproar of frenzied dancing meshed with the drum beat, and the sweaty knot of dancers rubbed and jounced indulgently against each other. Cheryl groaned as the woman in the leotard twirled and shimmered right in front of her. Then, spotting someone she knew on the edge of the floor, she gave me a quick thumbs-up gesture before wending her way through the feverish tangle. She bent her head, as she had when she spoke to me, and asked a plumpish woman to dance. The answer must have been yes; Cheryl took hold of the woman's belt loops, and slid down the woman's front, as gracefully as young sapling blood. When she shimmied back up, the greased ease of her muscles and her laughing mouth made me ache. I decided to get myself another beer.

Eyes played on me as I touched entryways through the packed bodies. Women shifted to let me pass. One woman caught her ring on my belt, apologized as she disengaged, and took advantage of the moment to fondle my crotch. I didn't mind, but I didn't invite her any further. When I reached the bar I commanded the bartender's attention and got me a beer. There was a hand on my ass. Turning my head, simultaneously moving out of range, I recognized Tanya.

"Where have you been keeping yourself?" she demanded, crowding her knee into mine.

"Working out, getting ready for the Gay Olympics."

"Are you still boxing?" She squeezed my left deltoid, admiring the meat.

I was half tempted to flex my pecs and have her feel them, and lowered my gaze to her breasts. Then I dropped my eyes to her mound, just the right size for my palm, but resisted trying out the fit.

"I sure wouldn't want to fight with you," she said, gliding her mound along the outside seam of my pants leg, not quite making contact but close enough to sear me with its heat. I figured she meant she would let me undress her.

I looked away, drank my beer. Her hand touched my solar plexus and I flinched.

"Come outside for a smoke?"

I agreed. She forged our way into the relative silence of the night. In the shadow of a nearby doorway, she lit up. The marijuana was sweet and strong in my lungs. Tanya let me unbutton the top button of her blouse. As I kissed her warm mouth, I stealthily undid her pants, and felt like a dog, excitedly maneuvering into position. I used my fingers to fuck Tanya while she held the last of the joint to my lips. Two women walked by but we paid them no mind. Tanya was too busy inhaling my smoke, gulping up my fingers; I jerkily thrust up inside of her until she came. Then I wanted to get inside her mouth, but she giggled against my chest as she straightened her clothes and I lost interest.

Cheryl was standing by the wall again when I finally returned to the dance floor. She noticed the color in my face and smiled knowingly. I liked having her body next to mine, the delicate breath of her flesh. I reached down and playfully hooked my finger inside her fly where the errant button had come undone. She didn't move. Her eyes filled my sight with their enormous, dark blue haze. Boldly, she deliberately lowered her gaze to my crotch. Such a fine, shapely face she had; sharp, angular bones and full lips. I envisioned her kneeling before me, and imagined my pleasure as I fucked her mouth.

Her long slender hands that play racquet ball so well pressed the wall behind her, holding back from holding me. We stood side by side, not quite breathing, for at least three songs. I wanted the boyish silky light in her eyes I'd seen when she measured my crotch with her gaze to contemplate sucking me. I could tell she wasn't really watching the other women, and finally asked,

"You want to go somewhere else?"

"OK," she said, and pushed herself away from the wall with eager enthusiasm.

Outside we paused to close our jackets. She didn't touch me, not even sitting behind me on my bike. She leaned back, her hands stuffed in her pockets. The ride was brief, a fast shot on the freeway, a few side streets, and I parked in front of her house. As soon as she'd unlocked the door and let me in, she threw her jacket on the couch and went to her stereo. She turned the music up loud and offered me something to drink. I'd picked up a polaroid camera from the arm of the couch and was examining it for film.

"What do you have?"

"Tequila."

I aimed the camera at her, located the loose jaunty angle of her hips in my frame, and pressed the shutter. Click, zip, the picture spat out. I fanned it in the air to dry.

"Tequila's fine."

We drank it out of shot glasses; tossed back the smooth fire, sucked a lemon to cut the heat, then licked salt to settle everything down. The picture of her crotch bloomed into full color in my hand. I skidded it across the coffee table for her to look at, pushed it the last few inches with my boot, and studied her face a minute before getting up and going into her bathroom. When I was through there, I found Cheryl had gone into her bedroom, and, claiming her shirt was sweaty, was in the process of changing it. I fetched the camera then stretched out on top of her bed to watch the action of her ribs sliding under her skin as she removed her shirt and pitched it to the back of her closet.

"Take off your jeans," I said, figuring I'd better make a move or we'd end up drinking and watching her VCR like we usually did.

She turned to look at me, her breasts small and inconsequential on an otherwise flat, sinewy chest.

"Leave your underwear on," I added, and laid one hand on my crotch to cup and warm myself. The gesture disturbed her. Immediately her nipples pricked up. Without removing her eyes from my hand rubbing myself, she stepped out of her tennies, undid her jeans and slipped them down over her butt. Her haunch hollowed out when she lifted her leg and drew her foot free.

"I want a picture of you with a bra on."

Hot blood pulsed high in her cheeks, then suddenly she seemed fuller, rounder; her breasts swelled; even her mound beneath her jockey briefs plumped up prettily. I wanted to jerk off, watching her tremble uncertainly then go to her dresser and take a lacy thing from the back of a drawer. She was clumsy putting it on for being unfamiliar with it, but she didn't let that stop her, and when it was fastened, turned around for me to see. Such a shy woman peeping out of her boyish form; the very sight of her made my voice go lower, my pecs swell, and my shoulders broaden with new strength. I stood to meet her, smoothed her hair, pressing my hot front to her belly. I stroked her winterlight skin, then urged her down on the bed, feeling along the sides of the frame for eye bolts I recalled she'd mentioned screwing in when she'd had a lover who wanted to be tied down.

That's what my slitted bandanas were for, wrists and ankles, quick restraints. I spread her legs and arms and secured her in that position, murmuring over and over, "You're my Girl, Baby, you're my Girl." When I stroked her with my crotch, she arched up to meet me with resilient, willing flesh and a mouth that was ready to eat me.

I resisted and picked up the camera. Standing over her, I pressed my boot to her cunt and aimed. Click. I drew back, aimed the camera eye at her lacy breasts, and click, shot again.

"K.C., let me have you. Let me suck you."

I soaked in the sight of her; all mine, my Girl. Her jockey briefs were wet clear through. I put the camera on the floor. The shots of her were on the bedspread, filling with color as I straddled her torso, slowly massaged the front of my jeans, then undid my fly. She wanted me like some kid wanting candy, big greedy eyes and wet lips. I pinned her shoulders with my knees, slid my fingers inside my jeans and brought them back out coated with cum. No sooner did I touch my thumb to her lips but she was sucking me in, drawing me down into her throat.

"Untie me," she begged. "I can do you better that way."

I undid her hands. She took my thumb back into her mouth, nibbled the underside of it, cupped my ass in her hands and set my

6

hips in motion. My belly went lean with each thrust, my thumb became more than it was meant to be; I went dizzy from the workings of her mouth and tongue, and with my free hand cradled her head as I fucked her face and came. Blood rushed into my face, then. The spasms gurgled low in my throat and emerged in strangled gasps and grunts.

I couldn't stop. I treated her roughly as I turned her over and entered from behind. Sweat dripped free of my short sleeves onto her ass as I humped her good and long and hard, and the pictures of her, striped by light coming through the venetian blinds, told the story.

Sweet Handle of Bone

Bo dressed in candlelight, with a glass of red wine on the dresser to help her along. When she bathed, she'd scrubbed her skin with a stiff bristle brush, and pretended it was someone else scratching her, preparing her for the party. Bo intended to have a good time. After rubbing styling gel into her hair, she blow-dried it perfectly, swept off her forehead and ducktailed in the back. Her roommate's red and black box of scented powder drew her gaze more than once. She knew how her roommate put it on, patting it into the folds of her belly, between her firm, plump thighs, and under her heavy hanging breasts where the blood veins showed blue. Girl stuff, Bo thought, then lifted the lid, poofed the soft pad in the powder and, feeling foolish, clumsily put some on her chest.

She dressed in the other room, occasionally tilting a sip of wine into her mouth, so red it was like blood, only thin and dry. It soothed her nerves. Candle shadows flickered on the wall, in Bo's face in the full length mirror. She moved about so the shadows danced at her arm then at her crotch, at her throat. She loved her throat, long and slim, like a statue, a nice dusty brown that looked all the darker next to her white overshirt.

A siren screamed outside. Bo peered around the edge of the bamboo curtain, but couldn't see anything out of the ordinary. The siren kept on going until it thinned into the distance and stopped. Suddenly, Bo was ravenous. She knew there wouldn't be any real food at the party, and went to the kitchen for a snack. The ceiling shade had broken the week before, and the bare bulb glanced relentlessly off all the shiny stainless steel in the room. Bo winced against the glare, carefully set her wine glass in the sink and took some leftover roast from the fridge. She stood next to the counter slicing thin strips then ate them. The knife was sharp, the meat faintly bloody; Bo cut a slice of bread, laid a piece of the red beef on it and chewed solemnly, blankly staring out the window at a bluish pool of streetlight.

There should be dyke gangs, she thought, patrolling the night; they'd come upon her in some very dark, out-of-the-way street, and just for the fun of it, surround her; a loose circle of them with black leather gauntlets and vests, staring her down. Snapping their fingers, murmuring and growling. They'd have whips at their belts; one of them would unwind hers, flick it playfully at Bo's crotch, never quite touching her, but enough to make her jump.

Bo shook her head and grinned sheepishly before finishing her sandwich in a few wolfish gulps and wiping her fingers on the towel hanging from the refrigerator door.

Outside it was misty, cool under the trees where Bo walked, thinking of herself as a panther, padding restlessly, quietly prowling the night. Laughing, she realized she'd missed the street she'd meant to turn on and doubled back through the alleyway. A dog came at her, choking on its own menace, making her leap to the left; her heart scudding high in her chest, she was relieved to have a fence between them, though it didn't look very strong. There was an overpowering smell of dog shit, and the dog's eyes gleamed as it slathered and snarled between the slats. Bo took off. It seemed like there were all sorts of things chasing her; the cobblestones tried to trip her, an old mattress with springs coming out its middle reached out to grab her. At the end of the alleyway she stood in the middle of the street to catch her breath, then checked out her hair in the rear view mirror of a car parked on the street. Opening her jacket to air her sweaty body, she set out again with jaunty step, determined she would make it with someone that night.

In the shade of a huge oak outside the party house, Bo rubbed each of her nipples then cupped her warm palm over her cunt. Thus prepared, she mounted the front stairs. Directly inside the door, she encountered two women going at it, mouth and tongues, fingers pinching and sliding, looking for openings into each others clothes. Bo pushed past them, stood in the doorway of the foyer, hitched her pants, twisted her black leather wristlet so the snap was on the underside of her arm, and made for the other side of the room where she'd spotted Kelly. She noticed a tall woman standing all alone, drinking beer, one boot flat to the wall behind her. Bo knew her slightly, she went by the initials, K.C., and was reported to have a mean temper.

Bo nodded quickly, uninvitingly, at May, an ex-lover, laid her jacket on a chair, and moved across the room where Kelly was talking to an outstandingly gorgeous woman.

"This is Yvonne," Kelly said, introducing Bo, who decided she was going to play this one cool.

The woman was just plain sexy, and as it turned out, recently returned from a year in Paris. Her skin was the color of toasted almonds, and her bobbed hair was black and silky.

"What were you doing in Paris?" Bo enquired, refusing Kelly's offer to get her a beer.

Yvonne's teeth were small, her lips inordinately red. There was something secretive about her that Bo liked as she listened to Yvonne explain about her parents moving to Paris for the year and that she'd decided to join them. She spoke with an accent. Her lips, when she smiled, lifted more on one side than the other, suggesting sarcasm; her eyes delivered a look so immediate, so fuckable, Bo got squirmy and wet, thinking about it.

Kelly returned with a beer for Yvonne, said worriedly, "Go get yourself something to drink Bo," but Bo wouldn't. She wanted to listen to Yvonne talk, and gaze at Yvonne's pointy tits, brazenly unfettered beneath the sweater she wore.

It wasn't that Yvonne was dressed in anything all that sexy, but she acted like she could take care of herself and had done it plenty; like she was used to catching a whole mess of wolf whistles wherever she went and simply shook them off with a toss of her silky clean hair.

"What're you doing in Seattle?" Bo asked, standing so close to Yvonne, their nipples almost touched.

"Just visiting," Yvonne replied, judging the face above her as very handsome, indeed. She glanced quickly over Bo's shoulder at K.C., at her bunched fist inside her front pocket.

Kelly told Bo she wanted her to meet someone.

"Later," Bo said. "How long are you going to be here?" she asked Yvonne, stumbling on her words because Yvonne had shifted her tit even closer.

"A couple of weeks. I live in Boston. You ever been to Boston?"

Bo shook her head. "I'm a Northwest Baby," she said, touching the front of her fly ever so lightly in the process of hitching her pants up.

Yvonne thought it would be good fun to let the blue-eyed Wonder Girl take her in a back room and fuck her, but as soon as she thought it, she shivered. Even across the distance of the room, she knew K.C.'s weighted stare; it brought her blood up, and a fresh cowgirl like Bo was suddenly much too pale for Yvonne's taste

"I heard someone mention cocaine," Yvonne murmured to Bo.

Kelly cast a nervous look in K.C.'s direction, unnerved by the intimate angle of Yvonne and Bo's heads.

"Do you know who has it?"

Bo didn't know, but didn't want to leave Yvonne in order to find out. But then Yvonne asked Kelly, and Kelly acted like Bo was the one should go talk to Flynn.

"I'm pretty sure she's got some," Kelly insisted, scanning the room and pointing Flynn out.

"Ok," Bo agreed irritably. "I'll be back," she promised, and, fortified by Yvonne's tit actually brushing her arm, went in search of some coke.

Flynn was no longer standing by the stereo. Bo didn't understand how a woman that big could disappear from a crowded room so fast. She looked in the kitchen, checked out both bedrooms, the foyer, and finally located Flynn on the back porch talking to a woman with bleached blonde hair. Flynn wasn't very tall, and very fat; smartly dressed in brown slacks and suspenders over a creamy silk shirt, with crummy run-down tennies on her feet. Bo waited impatiently for Flynn to finish her conversation, anxious to snort cocaine with Yvonne. Flynn looked up, irritated by the interruption.

"Flynn?"

Flynn acknowledged her name. The bleached woman excused herself, and Flynn sighed, watching her go.

"I hear you've got some cocaine," Bo said, gingerly resting her backside against the porch rail. It seemed strong enough to hold her up and she relaxed.

Flynn frowned, her face settled deeper into her double chin. "Who told you that?"

"Kelly."

"You want to buy some?" Flynn asked, shifting the grimy leather cap she wore lower over her eyes.

"Yeah."

"Do you want to try it first?"

Bo was getting cold and she wanted to get back inside, but Flynn had already taken a silver packet from her vest pocket and, setting it on the rail, carefully opened it. The porch light was so dim and yellow, Bo couldn't see the white powder Flynn crooned over. Bo leaned closer, was startled when Flynn touched the powder with the tip of her red red tongue, lizard like. Then she smacked her lips, took a little gold spoon from around her neck and solemnly handed it to Bo who completed the ritual by snorting a scoop into each of her nostrils. Sniffling a little to get the last of it up inside, she returned the spoon, swaying slightly as the first delicious quiver skittered up the back of her neck.

"Very nice," she murmured approvingly.

Flynn didn't smile. Her face was as intent as a bird watching a beetle. "You like that, hmmm?" She returned the packet to her vest pocket, withdrew a similar one from another pocket and held it out.

Bo had the impulse to grab Flynn's hand and kiss those plump fingers. Disconcerted by the absurd image of herself on her knees, Bo backed off and handed over her money.

"You didn't tell me your name."

Bo thought Flynn sounded like a gnome. She could be, her shoes were all muddy, as if she'd been tromping about in the woods, and her eyes were strange; she never blinked. A gnome; Bo grinned at the idea, then started laughing, and what with the coke skittering up and down her backbone, she couldn't stop. She lurched across the porch, sagged against the far wall, and when she straightened, rested her head on the dry, scaly boards so she could wipe the tears from her eyes.

Just that quick there was a blade at her throat.

Bo's laughter died instantly. "What do you want?" she rasped, frightened by the big, bone handled knife Flynn had in her hand, and by how light she was on her feet. All that weight and being so quick; maybe she was a gnome.

Flynn clucked reassuringly, slid the knife three inches to Bo's jugular vein, lightly pricking the dusky skin until a drop of blood welled to the surface. Her tongue darted out and licked it clean. Her musky smell had a calming effect on Bo. Still, Bo was afraid to speak or move, even when Flynn stroked Bo's cunt. Stroked it and stroked it, with unnerving heat, until Bo couldn't stand the exquisite pleasure, and would almost have preferred the blade through her throat. Then Flynn cut off Bo's shirt buttons, cut through her undershirt, leaving a red red track that stopped at the line of her jeans. Panting, she sheathed her knife, backed off a step then whirled about and vanished down the short flight of stairs and around the corner of the building.

Without thinking, Bo gave chase down a twisty back alley. A dog in a nearby sideyard broke into a frenzy of barking. Tree branches reached out and slapped Bo, but she paid them no heed. She hurdled a pile of rubbish and came up short when Flynn turned on her, her knife quivering at gut level. In the shadows, she looked mean.

"Hey, Baby, want some more?" Flynn crooned, motioning Bo closer as if coaxing a frightened horse.

Bo sidled in, though she didn't know why.

Flynn slammed her up against the brick alley wall so her head cracked and bled. It started to rain. The dog stopped barking. Bo was aware of the blade making an x on the skin over her heart; fingers undid her pants; she was certain Flynn was going to fuck her with the blade, but she couldn't fight. It was the gnome's odd, clucking voice that took it out of her. Dizzily, Bo realized it was bone, not blade, inside her cunt, filling out her belly until she'd never felt so good.

Finishing, Flynn fled. Bo slumped over on the wet ground, almost crying for the loss of that sweet bone handle. She heard footsteps, lifted her head up off the mucky ground and peered through the gloom. Yvonnne and her black-booted K.C. hurried past the alley mouth without looking in.

"Wait!" Bo croaked, staggering to her feet and doing up her fly. She hurriedly brushed herself off, swiped a hand through her hair and tied her shirt tails together in an effort to close up her shirt. She ran out of the alley even before she'd stopped to think what she was doing. The mist had gotten heavier. It beaded Bo's hair and watered the dried blood on her chest.

"Wait!" she yelled at the two women vanishing into the swirling mist.

Yvonne turned her head, gave one quick look over her shoulder, then threaded her arm through K.C.'s and hurried them along even faster.

Bo chased after, firmly clutching the silver packet she'd gotten from Flynn. She felt she'd never run faster. The clatter of her heels on the walk was all but swallowed up by the vaporous drizzle, but the sound of her breath pounded in her ears. She skidded on a patch of grass, turning the corner, and yelled again.

"Hey!"

K.C. broke away from Yvonne, stepped between her and the voice pursuing them. She frowned, her fists were cocked and ready. Bo trotted up, panting and more disheveled than she knew. Yvonne took in the bloody torn shirt, the visible x on Bo's muscled chest, and gave that one-sided smile of hers that had entranced Bo in the first place. Bo realized her disordered condition, and suddenly the episode with Flynn became real.

"What happened to you?" K.C.'s voice was sharp, disapproving.

"I cut myself." Bo started giggling, though she knew it was only a perverse reaction to K.C.'s overly Butch manner. "I'm not sure," she amended soberly, holding her shirt closed over the telltale x scratched into her skin with a real gush of longing for Flynn; she wished she'd run after her, instead.

"Here," Bo said, holding out the packet. "I got the coke you wanted."

Yvonne tossed her damp hair. Beads of mist glistened on her Mediterranean complexion. "It's too wet to do it here," she chided. "Maybe some other time."

Bo stared at her uncomprehendingly. She knew how Yvonne had looked at her back at the party, and wanted to open Yvonne's coat and put a hand on her pointy tits. She wanted to know how soft Yvonne's inner thighs were, and what she tasted like, cracked open.

"We could do it at my place. I just live a couple of blocks away."

Yvonne put her arm through K.C.'s. "Some other time," she warned evenly.

"You bought Yvonne some cocaine?"

"She asked me to," Bo flared, clutching herself in her own embrace. She was getting cold. K.C. glared at Yvonne who took her arm away and linked up with Bo.

"All right," Yvonne murmured drolly. "Lead the way."

Bo couldn't get her stride to match Yvonne's, and had to hippity-hop from time to time to even them out. Besides, K.C.'s sullen, violent need frightened her, and after two blocks, she tried to disengage from Yvonne on the pretext of tieing her shoe, but Yvonne told her to let it flop in a sexy, red lipped way. Bo's teeth started chattering. Yvonne held her closer. Their hips didn't quite fit, making their pace all the more ill-matched.

When they got to Bo's apartment, Bo gladly separated while she dug her keys out of her jean pocket and let them all in. K.C. stamped inside and stood like a menace in the corner with her arms crossed angrily across her chest.

"It's warmer in the kitchen," Bo stammered, dashing in there and flicking the light switch before remembering the broken shade. The glare was interrogatingly harsh. It made K.C. look sallow, and Bo noticed Yvonne's face was a bit pinched and worried by fatigue.

"Are you hungry?" she asked her guests, nervously yanking the refrigerator door open.

"Yvonne wants her desire," K.C. remarked snidely. She came up behind Yvonne, and though her face bore witness to a war going on inside, she merely placed her hands on Yvonne's shoulders and helped her out of her jacket.

Yvonne preened, fluffed her hair, and perched provocatively on the edge of the sink. Her plump lips revealed eager, sharp teeth when she wetted one finger and smoothed an eyebrow. "Do you have a mirror?" she asked promptingly.

Bo started out of her trance staring at Yvonne, closed the refrigerator, mumbled something about having one in the bathroom, and backed out of the room. Before she had completely exited she witnessed K.C.'s hand slicing the air then Yvonne's cheek. Yvonne whimpered excitedly as K.C. moved in on her, in on those pointy tits and hot, covered cunt, Bo wanted to protest, but knew she didn't have a chance. There was no mistaking the sluttish gaze Yvonne favored K.C. with, and the way she took K.C.'s hand and put it around her own throat. Then, when K.C. obligingly pinned her back against the cabinet, Yvonne undid her pants and shoved herself at K.C. who obliged once again.

Bo fled to the bathroom where the light was less stark and the big silver mirror showed her cut up shirt and chest to its full glory. Bo removed her tattered clothing and dropped it at her feet, then wonderingly studied the marks Flynn had made. She washed herself in a daze, recollecting that sweet bone handle inside her cunt. Lifting the red and black lid of the powder box, she dusted her scratches, her neck, her belly, then undid her jeans and watched in the mirror as she slowly parted her labia. She was disappointed to find nothing unusual. She'd almost expected to find Flynn's mark. Dreamily tracing the one on her chest, Bo touched her clitoral ridge. The chase came back to her, the way Flynn whirled around, knife ready. Bo rubbed herself a little harder. From the other room came sounds of Yvonne and K.C. fucking. Bo closed her eyes and imagined Flynn delicately teasing her clit with her knife, then turning the knife around and rotating the carved bone deep. Bo leaned against the wall which was Flynn's arms, and pushed two fingers inside.

The Fourth Errand

Molly wiped her mouth. "I'll be a little late this evening. I have some errands I need to do after work," she said, returning her napkin to her lap.

Beth looked up from the newspaper she was reading. "I've cooked three times this week already."

"I'll stop and get a pizza."

Beth poured herself another cup of coffee from the blue thermos jug on the table. "What errands?" she asked, returning to the editorial page.

"I have to go to the bank, and we need some toothpaste." Molly swallowed the last of her juice, pinched stray crumbs from the table and put them on her plate. "Then I have to pick up the book I ordered, and there's something else I need to get." She got up, brushed the wrinkles from her slacks and carried her dishes into the kitchen.

Beth hooked one arm over the back of her chair. The gold bracelet she wore glinted prettily on her wrist. Brushing her hair off her face with one grand sweep, she pursed her lips and waited with studied impatience for Molly to reemerge.

Naturally thin-lipped and severe, Molly's mouth was, however, suppressing a secretive smile when she paused in the kitchen doorway to squint at her glasses. She polished them with Beth's unused napkin, and put them back on, but not before Beth rapped her forearm with a fork and demanded, "What's the 'something else' you need to get?"

Molly picked vaguely at her shirt for imaginary lint, straightened her tie, and headed for the living room after noticing the time on her wristwatch. "Nothing much, just an errand." Her crisp, clipped words came back on Beth over Molly's shoulder. Beth jittered her foot against the table leg with true irritation as she attempted a calm perusal of the paper.

No sooner had Molly taken her blue blazer from the front closet and put it on than she remembered she'd forgotten her lunch, and in her precise, purposeful way, returned to the kitchen, crossing with held breath through Beth's icy aura. She rattled her lunch sack when she put her apple in, to let Beth know what she was doing, then paused once again in the kitchen doorway.

"Guess I'd better be off." She creased and recreased the folded down top of her brown paper sack.

Beth shrugged.

Molly felt her bowels contract; her wingtip shoes clacked across the clean dining room floor. Beth maintained a punishing silence until she heard the front door open, and Molly pick up her keys from the little mahogany table. Then she rose from her chair, breezed into the living room, leaving perfume in her wake.

"Goodbye," she said sarcastically, from across the room.

Molly rattled her keys against her leg, her eyes blinked behind their two round lenses, then she coughed suddenly, sharply into her cupped hand. Beth zeroed in on the jade plant by the door, checked its soil for dampness and clucked her tongue when she found it dry. Molly leaned in for a peck to Beth's cheek. Beth refused the ritualistic parting with an annoying habit she had of smirking and drawing back. But then she leaned against the doorjamb, so close to Molly, and with half closed eyes, Molly felt she was being invited into the bedroom.

Beth smiled archly, toyed with Molly's tiepin, confident she'd won hands down, that now Molly would reveal her silly secret.

"Goodbye," Molly said, and with superwoman effort actually turned and walked out the door without a plea for Beth's favor.

Beth's heart beat erratically; a temper tantrum for control reddened her face. Under the pretext of picking bugs off the plant on the porch, she watched Molly step briskly to her car and unlock it. Emanating incredulous, cool fury, Beth snapped part of the plant off. Molly arranged her briefcase and lunch on the car seat beside her with shortened breath and every one of her cells quivering for release; she'd know relief if only she'd trot back up the steps and submit to Beth's request. The lashing would be sweet and severe and short lived, but then, Oh God, Beth's scented lips on her own. Molly put the car in gear and drove off.

It was a long morning. Beth worked, but failed to concentrate more than a few minutes at a time on the legal research she was doing. She refused to allow Molly into her thoughts, but her burning fury didn't ebb, and her back itched something incredible, right between her shoulder blades. She finally resorted to rubbing up against the furniture like some animal. Somewhere along mid-afternoon, she found herself in the bathroom, brushing her teeth. When they were clean she fussed with her hair for a long time, combing it back then forward over her brow, eventually discovering a new way altogether; parted on the side and pinned back. She studied the change in her appearance, then took out her make-up and did her eyes. To top it off, she applied rouge to her lips. After blotting them, she freshened her blouse with several vigorous shakes as the grandmotherly clock in the living room struck five solemn notes, then impressed her perfect lips on the looking glass.

Through with her work for the week, Molly waited for a green light before crossing the street with an unusually jaunty step. She was almost carefree as she bought toothpaste, picked up her book and waited in the bank line. Even driving up to Capitol Hill in rush hour traffic didn't daunt her spirits. She ordered a pizza at Piecora's, then walked a few blocks to a nearby shop. Hesitating briefly to adjust her tie, she went it. A bell on the door announced her arrival. The place was painted white. Most of the items were black leather.

Molly nodded curtly when the proprietress greeted her. She was thankful there was another customer so she could look around without interruption. There were fancy leather restraints in a glass case, things for pinching the nipples, black dildos and tit rings. Molly kept her hands buried deep in her pockets and gazed without expression at a display of whips on the wall. She overheard something about a sheath and saw out of the corner of her eye a large, bone-handled knife pass between the customer and the shop owner. Stepping closer to the whips, Molly touched one. She was surprised at how soft it was. Her cunt warmed and a secret smile flickered over her mouth as she rubbed her sweaty palm against the lining of her pocket.

Shortly thereafter she left the shop carefully carrying an oblong box as if it had a live thing it it. She kept thinking of it as a snake, and almost forgot the pizza. When she pulled in the driveway of her and Beth's home, it was already dark. Summoning courage, she ascended the steps and went inside.

Beth was on their new, white couch, reading. She finished the paragraph she was on before she deigned to look up, and then only long enough to snort a miffed humph before she went back to her book. However, the box in Molly's arms hadn't escaped her notice and inwardly she warmed a little, thinking Molly had bought her a present. Marking her place with a finger, she yawned, showing her gold and silver fillings.

Molly put her briefcase and the pizza on the little mahogany table, shuffled through the mail and found nothing worth immediate attention, placed the box in the chair that matched the couch, and hung her blazer up. "How was your day?" she asked, watching Beth for signs of temper.

Beth yawned again. "Fine."

Moving a little closer, Molly loosened her tie, swallowed deeply and stammered, "You look wonderful tonight. Your hair looks nice that way."

Beth gave a small snort through her nose as way of appreciation, and without looking at Molly asked where the pizza was from.

"Piecora's. Is that all right?"

"What were you doing on the hill?"

Molly said, "I'll warm up the pizza and change." She hurried out of the room. Beth heard her go upstairs into their bedroom; heard the closet door swish across the carpet. She tapped her front tooth with her index finder as she speculated on what was in the box, then settled back into her book with a smug look on her face until Molly called her to the table.

They ate without speaking. The clock chimed the half hour. Molly finished her beer, then, because she felt some kind of celebration was in order, got herself another.

"Aren't we being daring tonight!" Beth announced mockingly. "What's the occasion? Maybe I should have another one, too."

Molly got one and poured it for her, then cleared the table. By the time she got back to the dining room, Beth had relocated to the couch. Molly took a deep breath and joined her. They sat on either end of the couch not looking at each other. Molly kept her eyes on the box, Beth examined her nails. Because of the gift, she was prepared to forgive Molly, and didn't think of it as giving in when she said, "All right, what's in the box?" She tucked her legs beneath her and tugged her skirt down over her knees.

Molly presented it to her.

"Is it for me?" Beth feigned innocently and charming surprise.

"Yes. Well, kind of," Molly amended, sitting very upright and still.

Beth slowly opened the box and lifted a piece of white tissue paper. For a long time she did nothing. Finally Molly reached in and took out an exquisitely fashioned, black leather whip, a couple of feet in length.

"Feel it," she said.

Beth prissed her mouth, poked it with the tip of her finger, shocked by the quality of reverence in Molly's voice. "What's it for?"

"It's a whip."

"I know that, but what did you get it for?"

"You."

Beth's cheeks flushed hot beneath her make-up. "Could you scratch my back?" she retorted angrily, twisting around so Molly could reach it.

Molly freed Beth's blouse from her skirt and slid the handle of the whip up underneath to do as she was told.

Beth gasped not so much from relief of her itch but from the warmed leather on her skin. Then she turned on Molly, and was silenced by the way Molly sat stroking the black braid. Her mouth was actually relaxed, which put her nose into a whole new perspective; it looked almost noble, and her eyes were dreamy.

"Feels so good," Molly said, lifting the whip's lash and letting it fall across Beth's leg. "Touch it some more."

"I don't want to."

"Well, I want you to."

There were nasty glints of scorn and ridicule in Beth's eyes, but just as she opened her mouth to vent them, the look Molly gave her made her close it again. She'd never seen a look quite like it coming from Molly, and quivered with fine prickles of shame. She felt she was falling as she laid a hand on the braided leather.

"That's right."

Beth closed her eyes and fingered the entire length. "What are you going to do with it?" she asked in a small, girlish voice.

Molly played the tongue of the whip on Beth's nipples, then pushed her skirt up with the thick handle; when the skirt wouldn't go any further, Molly used the handle for a probe.

"No," Beth whispered, thoroughly ashamed for untucking her legs and rucking her skirt up to her waist.

Molly stood right in front of Beth, dangling the whip, switching it back and forth so the tongue flicked Beth's white thighs. Beth couldn't bear to watch; how guttural, how squalid of her, wanting to throw herself at Molly's feet and kiss them!

Molly snapped the whip lightly on tender skin. Beth's eyes opened to Molly, never quite so handsome, what with the sleeves of her old pink oxford shirt rolled up, and her knees not really bowed and weak, but sturdy, flexing as she raised the whip and brought it down. Beth half slid off the couch, moaning that she'd be Molly's Jezebel.

Molly stared at Beth, her cheek on Molly's old, worn slipper, writhing for more. "Take off your blouse," she barked, momentarily frightened of her new role. Beth practically ripped the cloth away then groveled again on the rug. Molly experienced something fierce; something nearly mean brought her hand up and the whip down on her lover. Beth cried out with anxious humiliation.

"I'll do anything you want me to," she moaned. Her hair had come unpinned. Her scented cleavage and crumpled skirt roused the soiled temptress in her. She grabbed Molly's crotch, a crass, gross act that made her wild with imagined debauchery. "I'm yours," she panted, wanting her rump spanked and Molly to mount her as if she were nothing more than a dog.

The clock whirred and began its hourly chime. Molly's lips were nearly full with unaccustomed blood. She was stronger than ever she'd known. It made her taller; she no longer felt pale. She experimentally laid her precious whip up and down Beth's back, then pushed Beth's skirt all the way up and lowered her panties to her knees. Beth whimpered. The sound whipped Molly's blood to conquest level.

Beth gazed wide-eyed back over her shoulder. Molly wanted to slap Beth, give the punishment that was asked of her, but she'd never slapped anyone before. Her palm was hot to do it, and she gave it a try, flooding them both with horror and shame and lust. Beth wriggled her butt higher in the air. She couldn't speak the words, but she wanted to be spanked. Tying her whip around her waist, Molly positioned herself to paddle Beth's ass with her hand.

"What have I done?" Beth cried in sullied piteous moans.

"You're a bitch, aren't you?"

"Yes. What are you going to do with me?"

"Spank you just like you deserve."

"You're going to beat me?"

Molly raised her head, groping for familiarity. Was this their living room? Usually by this time they had the television on, but it was blank and grey. Molly touched the crack of Beth's ass, then parted it, moistened her finger and circled the tiny puckered hole.

"No!"

"Yes."

Beth sagged into the desperate pleasure weighing her down, then jerked to attention as Molly's hand smacked her ass simultaneous with penetration. Each tentative painful thrust was tempered by a smack so Beth didn't know which punishment was which. It's wicked, it's dirty, she thought, coughing out her breath like she imagined an animal would do as it was fucked.

Molly smacked Beth's ass good as the handle of the whip dangled down and banged into Beth's clit and her deep riding finger explored new ways of making Beth come. When she screamed, they were momentarily daunted out of concern for neighbors, but Molly felt reckless, careless, and continued with more heat than ever.

"No more, Molly, please, it's starting to hurt."

High shame burned in Molly's heart that she hadn't known. She withdrew. Her finger was soiled. Beth looked sodden and spineless on the rug, her panties around her knees, hand marks on her ass. Molly knelt down, clumsily stroked Beth's back as she cleaned her finger on the cuff of her pants.

"You ok?"

Beth didn't say anything. The rug smelled of shampoo. There were dust balls under the chair; Molly's hand on her back. A tight rumble low in Beth's stomach erupted into her throat. She gulped and sobbed. Tears rushed clean to her eyes. Molly curled up right alongside her, murmuring over and over, "I love you, Bethy, I love you."

Friday Night at Lacey's

In the back room bar, fish with long wavy tails and fins sucked at the glass of three large aquariums. Jane was on her second shot of tequila, lemon slices and a shaker of salt were in front of her, as well as a schooner of dark beer for a chaser. Whitsun drank her tequila mixed with orange juice, and Shannon had ordered vodka, straight up.

First they made a toast to "D" shift, the shift they worked, then they toasted the Fire Department with much mock sincerity and sarcastic guffawing, though underneath they were serious, as serious as their muscled shoulders and the fires they'd fought. They were big women, even Whitsun, who was slight of body.

Shannon slouched back in her seat and gazed at the ceiling, jiggling her foot restlessly.

Jane twiddled a red plastic stir stick, pointed it at Shannon and solemnly confided in Whitsun, "Shannon hasn't had enough sex lately."

Shannon snorted through her nose.

"We should do something for her," Jane concluded, clearing her throat and smiling encouragingly at Shannon who laughed and lightly shoved Jane to make her stop. "See? She's an animal! What are we going to do?" Jane quavered, desperately clutching Whitsun's arm.

Whitsun smiled, cast a sliding side glance at Shannon sprawled in her seat, her blue shirt partially off one shoulder, showing her very white tee shirt and part of her chest. "I don't know," Whitsun said calmly controlling her face of all reaction, and displacing Jane's hand from her arm under the guise of reaching for her drink. Briefly her eyes met Shannon's, slid away.

Shannon ordered another vodka though she didn't really want it.

"Let's go see a belly dancer!" Jane said, brightening considerably. "I know of a good one, over at that Greek restaurant on Pike."

Whitsun shook her head, lit a cigarette and blew the smoke sideways, away from them.

"Can I bum a cigarette?" Shannon asked, reaching for the pack.

"You guys are a lot of fun," Jane complained, frankly resting both forearms on the table and looking from one to the other. "We could go to my house and have a threesome," she suggested.

Shannon thought it was a joke, and gave Whitsun an eye-rolling conspiratorial grin through the smoke she exhaled. The look, innocent and slightly smoky, pierced Whitsun clear through. She coughed and concentrated on stubbing out her cigarette. She had had an affair with Jane when she first joined the Fire Department, and knew all about Jane's fancies. However, she didn't know Jane had been eyeing Shannon.

Jane sighed at the futility of it all and gazed morosely into her beer glass.

"What about Lacey's?" Whitsun suggested lamely, feeling vaguely responsible for Jane's irritability.

"Might as well, there's certainly not much action here," Jane complained mildly.

Shannon took some gum from her jacket pocket, unwrapped it and folded it into her mouth. "Want some?" she asked Whitsun who was looking at her.

Whitsun declined, though, yes, of course, she wanted gum; the piece in Shannon's mouth, to be exact. The one with her spit chewed into it. Whitsun distracted herself with her chapstick, applied it thoroughly to both lips.

"That's what we'll do then," Jane decided aloud. "We'll go to Lacey's. Maybe we'll be lucky, maybe they've got something hot going on tonight."

"Yeah, if we're lucky," Shannon laughed, suddenly cheerful. "At least there'll be a roomful of women. She undid her belt and retucked her shirt.

"This isn't a bathroom," Jane declared, gawking unashamedly.

Shannon turned partly around and grabbed her own ass; "Might as well have some of this while you're at it," she drawled in an effort to act the part and be funny.

"Oooh! This girl is hot! Let's get out of here before I start humping her right here!"

Shannon went slightly red which made Jane hoot all the more.

Self consciously cinching and buckling her belt, Shannon stood up and made for the door behind Jane, then turned back and grabbed Whit by the shoulder. "Come on, let's go. What are you waiting for?"

Whit was studying the fish, their sucking mouths on the glass prison. "Just looking at the fish," she replied, going hot all over from Shannon's brief grip on her shoulder. She followed Shannon out of the bar. It's no different than going into a fire, she thought, gazing at Shannon's muscled haunches. Just keep a level head.

Out on the street, Jane linked arms with her companions and sang in a husky, bawdy voice, "It's me in the middle, just me in the middle, and I hope to God it stays that way!"

Whitsun was embarrassed, and just a little peeved, then, because she pulled away and lagged behind attending to her shoelace, she was forced into the outside position again when they crowded into Shannon's truck.

"This is going to be fun," Jane exclaimed, straddling the stick shift, squirming and making raucous sounds when Shannon shifted into reverse, right up her thigh.

Whitsun kept an aloof exterior; gazed out the window at a fantasy of herself fucking Shannon's gearshift, the back shiny knob at the tip, while Shannon lounged in the seat, smoking and watching. She wouldn't get it right, Shannon would have to jerk her up close and slap her a few times, make her try it again, until all of the knob disappeared inside.

"Whit!" Shannon said for the second time.

Jane tickled Whitsun in the ribs.

"What?" Whit snapped, much more flustered and annoyed than she wanted to admit.

Shannon raised one surprised eyebrow, widened her blue eyes to accent her sincere intentions and asked, "Can I bum another cigarette? I'll buy you a pack tomorrow."

Whit handed one over, all too conscious of Jane silently studying her. She knew Jane had guessed the truth. Shannon shifted into first, pulled away from the curb, then leaned across Jane to switch the radio on. Their ride across town was orchestrated by Stevie Wonder singing "I was made to love her," loudly accompanied by Jane-In-The-Middle who pressed her plump thighs against the leg on either side of her without any pretense at subtlety.

Lacey's was in a rundown neighborhood, with a small sign over the door. Inside, a large mirror directly faced the door. Whitsun avoided it, Jane made fun of her weight as she adjusted her clothes, but she was only paying some kind of lip service, for her eyes had the shine of self approval in them, and she clapped her cupped palm against her stomach as she might a very dear friend. Shannon combed her hair, experimented with her collar up, then down, was about to comb her hair again when Jane poked her head back through the doorway and called,

"Come on, Hotstuff!" She disappeared into the next room.

"How's it going?" Shannon asked the woman collecting money.

"Great. You're in for a good show tonight."

"Yeah?"

"It's going to be wild," the woman promised.

Shannon stuffed her change into her back pocket, nodded, then went into the main room where she found Jane and Whitsun at a table near the front of the stage. She was about to sit next to Jane, but Jane lunged up out of her chair and insisted Shannon sit next to Whitsun. "I'm going to be doing some networking," she exclaimed as explanation, lewdly craning her neck to get a good look at who all was there, winking at Whitsun as Shannon maneuvered into the abandoned chair. Whitsun didn't appreciate Jane's candid interference and looked away, though she was thankful for the seating arrangement.

Jane waved at Mandy, another city employee, on the bureaucratic end, then noticed Molly was at the same table, and quickly looked the other way. Dory was seated near the back. "Dory's here!" she whispered loudly. "What do you want to bet I make it with her tonight!" She laid her hand palm up on the table, and when her friends wouldn't bet, guffawed and sauntered off.

After several long moments Whitsun observed, "I've never seen it so busy here."

"I know, it's packed," Shannon agreed, signaling the waitperson who looked as if she were still in her teens. Shannon nudged Whitsun's knee with her own, then growled her appreciation as the waitperson approached their table with a loose limbed, almost sullen saunter. She waited for their order, one leg thrust out, her cunt practically in Shannon's face.

Shannon wanted to eat it. "Beer," she mumbled, then somewhat louder, "Whit? What do you want?"

"Beer," Whit answered dismissingly, looking the other way.

"Did you see that?" Shannon crowed, all but done in by the sexy butt switching off across the room. She groaned and laid her brow on Whitsun's shoulder, but only briefly, for someone else caught her eye. She twisted around to get a better view.

Whitsun took out her lip balm and shakily applied it.

"God, look at Jane," Shannon pointed her out, comfortably seated between Dory and someone else, with a third woman on her lap.

Whitsun laughed outright, pleased to see Jane engaged elsewhere, obviously for the evening. "Guess she's deserted us," she said, glancing over at Shannon to see if she was pleased.

"Can I borrow one more cigarette?" Shannon asked. Whitsun took her time removing it from the pack so's to keep Shannon's eyes on her, then lit it, and was about to ask about the scar on Shannon's cheek when their beer arrived and the dance music stopped. A woman stepped up onto the stage and waited for the milling and chatter to cease before she said, "Tonight we have someone who's just moved here from Denver."

There were a few cheers from the crowd.

"She's got quite an act for you."

A wolf whistle sliced through the room, then there were shouts of laughter as Jane yelled, "And are we ever ready!"

"So, without any further delay, let's welcome, Ms. Laba!"

The announcer parted the heavy velveteen curtains and went backstage.

"Well, where is she?" someone quipped after a moment or two.

Someone else started stomping her feet; more women stomped their feet, and those who knew how, whistled with their fingers between their teeth. "Ms. Laba! Ms. Laba! Ms. Laba!" went the chant as the energy in the room mounted. Shannon joined right in, exuberantly stamping her boot on the wood floor.

The velveteen curtains swayed as someone took hold from backstage. Then a woman thrust the curtain wide at the center and stepped through, bringing the house to momentary silence; maybe the women were only catching their breath, for after the brief silence, the room was split open with whistles and outcries.

Ms. Laba smoked her audience with a naked saunter to center stage, set the black leather suitcase with the tiny twinkling silver studs she was carrying down, and straddled it, lightly rubbing her cunt along the upright handle.

"Will someone," she said huskily, leveling her audience with her immodest gaze, "bring me a chair?"

Shannon sat at the edge of hers as if waiting for the first puffs of smoke before she charged in to lock the fire, waited too long, however, mesmerized by the twat on the upright handle, and lost her chance. Another woman carried her chair to Ms. Laba, and was well rewarded with some cum for her lips.

Ms. Laba bent over the chair, showing the crack of her ass and the soft spume shooting out below. The sight of Ms. Laba's ass, the way she reached around and played with her crack, treated her audience to a view of her asshole, did something to Shannon's stomach. Sitting proper on the chair, Ms. Laba opened the suitcase and unpacked a pair of red heels. She licked one of the spikes before drawing it down her front, while twiddling a gold ring in her left nipple with her other hand. The spike left a red mark, clear into her bush, then she was fucking herself with it, but she was only teasing; she wasn't going to let them see her come, and wagging the spike at them lasciviously, licked it clean.

Shannon glanced sideways at Whitsun who sat staring straight ahead, thinking how much she wanted to be the one on stage, with Shannon watching her, coiled and tense.

Ms. Laba put the heels under the chair, took a pair of silk panties from the suitcase and smelled them, sucked the cotton crotch, put a finger up inside herself and sucked that before raising it in the air, calling attention to a slow version of a strip tease coming from backstage. Twirling her panties over her head while watching her audience with come hither eyes and moistened lips, Ms. Laba began flicking herself all over with the silken underthing, then slowly, smiling wickedly, drew them up over her legs and covered up her cunt.

The brazen strut of the music was illogical, lazily careening towards the final bump and grind, when Ms. Laba was busy putting her skirt on. Her large, full breasts hung down before her as she, like a fine horse pricking its heels, flexing each slender ankle into the hand of the groom, stepped into her skirt and skimmed it up around her waist. She fastened it while her hair tumbled, clean and shot with gold red, about her face; closed her eyes and slid both hands down the slinky shiny fabric, inviting them no more. Somewhere in the room someone groaned.

Shannon wanted to rip the skirt off. She felt cheated, taunted by the ribald music promising her everything would come off when it wasn't true. Whitsun scooted her chair a few inches closer to Shannon's, until their sleeves touched. She like the way Shannon's hair was shaved in the back, bringing the hairline to a point. On impulse, she touched the shaved part, shivering from the contact and the smooth shiny feel of Shannon's skin. Shannon tensed alert under the tentative touch, but it was gone before she could pay it much mind.

On stage, Ms. Laba donned a black leather harness, turning away from the audience, she snugged it, then faced them again with captured breasts, the nipples very erect. She clipped a thin gold chain to the ring in her tit, the other end to a ring on the harness, and slipped a silk garment over her head. It bloused and covered her; she was dressed. Ever so slowly her hips began to undulate; soon she was dry humping, thrusting her mound at them, pulling it back, thrusting as the lights dimmed. She put her heels on, the muscles in her calves taut and powerful. The harness looked like a brand under the silk, and the music quickened into the final drum roll, that rousing bit that means the g-string is about to come off. Ms. Laba played with her hat, then put it on her head with a flourish, and strode off stage, her back compelling a hundred cunts and a hundred throats to call after her.

Whitsun started from her chair as an impassioned lament filled the room; women were literally panting on their feet, pounding the tables and clapping their hands for more. Shannon was not alone in wildly looking about for someone she could have. As if on cue, the lights went out. Whitsun reacted immediately, with more aggressive adrenaline than she'd ever used at one single fire, and jumped Shannon, pinning her to the floor. There was a mad scramble in the room as cunts were undone and quickly had. Whitsun plunged her tongue into Shannon's mouth. She tasted of beer; she sucked Whit's tongue until it hurt. Whit took hold of Shannon's chin and forced her to let up, then tore Shannon's shirt in an effort to keep her subdued. Whit heard the cloth give, the grunt Shannon gave in response. Knowing there was little time, she locked Shannon's wrists to the floor and dry humped her, hoping she was rubbing their clits together; at least her own clit was rubbed, and thinking of nothing else, she concentrated on the heat spasming through her belly and fanning into her cunt, eventually making her toes curl and her breath gurgle in her throat. She came quickly, but then, she'd been cocked and loaded for so long, and the spillover into her underwear was all the more delicious for the fact that she was able to keep Shannon down.

The lights came back up on a giggling, sheepish crowd. Whitsun was standing, applying balm to her bruised lips. Shannon came up off the floor in slow motion, eyed Whit with puzzled, narrowed eyes, then examined her torn shirt. Whitsun smiled to herself and looked around the room for Jane.

Danielle's

North was at least an hour late, and it put me in a bad mood. "Where've you been?" I demanded as soon as she walked in the door. "You know I wanted to be at the gym by five. It closes in an hour, and today's my long work-out day."

"I know," North said placatingly, staying out of my reach. "But I got us a room at Danielle's."

"How did you manage that?" I asked, not quite ready to be mollified. Danielle's was the new women's gym in town, very elite; not a place I'd ever thought to find myself in.

Nor picked up my jacket from the couch and held it out to me. "I'm sorry I was late."

I took the jacket from her, rammed my arms into the sleeves and grabbed up my bag all in the same motion. "Danielle's better be good," I warned gruffly, and preceded North out of the house.

She drove, glancing at me now and then, but I ignored her, even pointedly craned my neck to get a second and third look at a woman we passed by on our way downtown, as way of letting North know I could do without her. She parked in Danielle's underground lot and we took the elevator to the sixteenth floor. The place was plush, carpets on the walls, even, the color of creamy cum, very comforting. I waited while North had her pleasure handling pertinent matters at the front desk; she was businesslike, with just the right touch of friendliness. I liked the easy manner in which she took her wallet from the inside pocket of her sports coat, paid, then picked up our room key. I suspected she'd paid a tidy sum, but I didn't ask. However, I felt much kinder towards her as we walked along one silent corridor, turned right into another, then stopped in front of room thirteen. She moved in front of me to open the door.

I admired the slim line of her back, bent over her and kissed the tender part of her neck. She turned to me with a smile.

"You think it's going to be that easy, huh?" I put a hammerlock around her throat, and using my weight to pin her against the door, tilted her head so her neck was exposed to my teeth. I bore down until her unruffled, highly efficient manner stirred and broke under the pain. "You like that? Think you deserve more?"

She gasped and nodded.

"I'm not so sure. You kept me waiting, you know."

"I know. I'm sorry. Please . . ."

"Please, what?" I made sure no one was coming along the corridor, and keeping her flattened to the door with my hips, took a leather thong from my pocket.

She pressed her cheek tight against the wood grain, and with furtive side glances tried to watch what I was preparing to do.

"I told you, quit looking at me." I smacked her butt hard to make sure she was listening. She closed her eyes and turned quivery, all over anxious to please. "That's better." I quickly fashioned a double loop and secured her hands behind her.

"Maybe I'll just leave you here like this. Someone's bound to come along and want you." I stood off from her, wanting her to feel abandoned.

"Teddy, please!" She trembled before me with bowed head and bound wrists, a sight I couldn't resist.

I reached around to her front and opened her fly with one downward sweep, then roughly lowered her pants down over her ass.

"Too public for you?" I asked mockingly.

"No," she assured me, thrusting her ass into my hand. "I want you to take me."

I moistened my finger. Movement at the other end of the hallway caught my eye; three women had just turned the corner and were approaching. I hesitated, then not about to share her with anyone, smartly slapped Nor on the ass. "That's enough for now," I hissed, slipping her pants up and untieing her hands. She protested. I indicated the three women almost upon us, but could tell North didn't think they were enough reason to stop.

"Let's go in the room," she begged, but I flickered my hand at her, letting her know I was irritated and didn't want to hear any more. She fumbled with her fly as I eyed the women.

They were dressed in shorts and tee shirts, white crew socks and clean tennies. The smallest of the three, her arm muscles still pumped from her work-out, advanced ahead of her companions, came directly at me and without so much as a word of greeting, went to her knees with the smoothest quad action I'd ever seen, and began kissing my boots. There was no time to be surprised. I acted instinctively, looped my thong around the woman's neck and pulled her head back. What a mouth; eager to kiss, lick, suck, whatever I might ask. I squeezed off her breath with my leather, and was amazed to see she only wanted more. Straddling her, I bent her arm up behind her back so her shoulder joint was stretched to the point of dislocation.

"It's all yours," she whispered from that haze where pain drugs the mind and cunt with pleasure.

I stroked her hamstrings and the bit of cunt hair curling from her shorts. Someone coughed loudly. With my hand on my slave's hindquarters, I looked up at two new arrivals. They were tall, heavy women dressed in expensive suits. Both of them had clipped haircuts and a powerful girth. I pulled my slave to her feet and casually rubbed the circulation back into her arm.

"Hey, Van, found yourself a good one, eh?"

The woman I'd been about to fuck laughed lazily.

I let her go, figuring I might be trespassing. The tallest of the lot, the one with the briefcase, appraised me blatantly, then gave a curt nod and led the entire group across the hall into the room opposite. I could hear them, behind the closed door.

"Where did you come up with her, Van?"

"There she was, tying up that woman, and you know how I am."

There was low, excited laughter, the sound of a slap, another, and Van moaning for more.

With pursed lips, North unlocked our door and went in. I closed it then leaned against the wall to watch her turn on the lights, check the heat and open the curtains. I knew she was agitated by the way she moved; she snapped the curtains wide then remained by them, staring out at the city.

"North, Christ, it's no big deal!" I muttered roughly, joining her at the window, thinking I'd make amends by fucking her in front of the view.

There was a knock at the door. It opened and Van, the two heavy women, came in.

"Hi," Van said cheerfully, with eyes only for me. "This is Robyn." She indicated the woman who had been carrying the briefcase. "And Slo."

I bobbed my head, acknowledging each introduction. "I'm Teddy and this," I pulled North up alongside me, "is North." I petted North's ass then plopped down on the couch, inviting North to sit with me. She perched on the arm.

Van sprawled invitingly on the chair opposite. Robyn paced, stopped, pressed me with a look. "There might be some money in you," she said shrewdly, cocking her head to one side and narrowing her eyes.

I rolled that over in my mind. Nor stroked my trapezius where it inserted into my neck. I accepted the caress. Soon her entire hand was rubbing my upper back, making me uncomfortable, but I let it be for the time being.

"You interested in working for me as a Top?"

"How much money?"

Robyn looked amused, glanced at Slo, and started pacing again. Van stretched luxuriously. My cunt responded accordingly.

"We'll see how it goes," Robyn said. "I'd set you up, take my cut for managing. Eventually I want to have a house, but for now we'd use this place." Her handsome hands gestured expansively.

I grinned, turned to see Nor's response and found her tolerantly picking lint off the couch. I slapped her knee a couple of times to reassure her we were still on for later.

"Van, come here," Robyn said, snapping her fingers without taking her eyes off me.

Slo shifted forward in her chair as Van did what she'd been told.

"Undress for this woman and give yourself to her."

While we watched, Van settled into a kind of trance as she slowly undressed. When she was naked, she went to the floor, and crawled to a position at my feet. Robyn took a position close by, breathing loudly through her mouth. I hardened inside as I yanked Van to me then flung her at Robyn, quickly covering her from behind. Robyn pressed Van's head down into the opening of her pants, making her suck cunt while I teased Van's ass into accepting me. I took my time though I was rough about it, slapping, pinching and grabbing. I wanted her to gush out onto the floor. I heard Slo's zipper snick open; Robyn gurgled and as she was about to come, I brought Van to a simultaneous climax, then shoved up into the lining of her ass and rode her until I was out of my senses. Never once did I lose contact with Van, though; it was as if we were streamlined together. Robyn's hand on my shoulder brought us back. I lowered Van to the floor and petted her while the room shifted and returned to normal.

Sitting on my heels, I noticed Robyn exchange a long look with Slo before reaching down and stroking Van's hair. Considering me, she said, "Meet you in the weight room in fifteen minutes."

"Yeah, ok," I agreed, and as soon as they left, turned to North who'd gotten up and was again standing by the window. "Think I checked out ok?" I asked, though I wasn't really worried. It was pretty clear that working out together was a way of clinching the deal

"Hey," I said coaxingly, putting my arms around North. "They're going to pay me good money."

She didn't say anything. I got irritated. She knew that I didn't always want her paying for everything. "We've got all night," I reminded her. "Just think how good it'll feel, once these muscles of mine are all pumped up."

She sighed to let me know I was asking a lot, but I was already absorbed in changing my clothes. I was a little nervous thinking about matching Robyn and Slo, who looked as if they lifted heavy weights, but I just clenched my jaw and told North to hurry up so we wouldn't be late. I liked to have her nearby when I worked out;

she spotted me when I needed it, and admired my efforts. I rushed her through the hallways to the weight room, then paused before going in, pretending to rub a cramp in my leg. North understood, though; she quit her sullen air and told me I'd do just fine. I smiled gratefully then pushed on ahead.

The room was larger than I had hoped, with polished wood floors and full length mirrors on most of the walls. There were abundant free weights, Nautilus and Universal machines, a series of chin-up bars and one big mat to stretch out on, as well as a squatting station and a cross pull set up. There were three other women working out. The one doing flys on a nearby bench was something else. She was slight of build, which made her muscular definition all the more impressive, I thought, momentarily agog with the bulges alive under her smooth, brown skin as she grunted up the last two reps. Dropping the heavy dumbbells on the floor, she sprang up from her bench and examined herself in the mirror. Her veins were gorged with blood and exertion, and beneath her tee shirt with the words, Seattle Firefighter, across the front in red, she was pumped to hulk proportions.

I rolled my sleeves to better show my biceps, and crossed the room to the bench press, where I always started my work-out, just as North always started by stretching. I'd just gotten myself situated on my back, and had pressed the bar directly above me, when Robyn and Slo came in. I pretended not to see them, until I finished my first set, wanting them to see me in action. Then, carefully setting the bar in its upright stirrups, I sat up, flushed with my first exertion. They were dressed more casually than before, but certainly not for a work-out. I was perplexed when Slo approached the other three women working out and said something to them, causing them to pick up their gear and leave.

"Aren't you guys going to work out?"

"You go ahead," Robyn told me firmly.

Slo grabbed a fifty pound barbell in her left hand and executed a few easy curls, replaced it and picked up a sixty-pounder in her right, did a few more.

The situation made me uneasy. I sought out North, but she was used to leaving me alone to my work-outs, and was busy with her sit-ups.

"Come on, Kid," Robyn said. "Let's get a look at you."

I added ten pounds to my bar, laid back down and took a good grip on the bar.

"I'll spot you, ok?" Robyn said, standing so the V of her inner thighs was just above my face.

I puffed my chest, took my time adjusting my grip, then did eight repetitions without a hitch. "Add another ten, would you?" I said, proud of myself.

Robyn took off each collar, added five pounds to either side, tightened the collars, then stood ready while I did another eight. My arms quavered getting it up the last two times. Robyn took the bar, set it in place, and said as if stating a fact, "Ten more pounds?"

"No, five."

"Let's go ten. You can do better than this."

Slo stood at my feet squeezing a rubber ball to strengthen her grip. "Robyn'll get you in shape," she said wickedly.

"I am in shape," I protested heatedly.

Slo tapped my biceps, leered at me and said, "That's not the kind of shape I mean." She bounced the ball on the bench between my legs then swatted my knee.

"What does she mean?" I asked Robyn, rising and twisting around to look at her.

She pushed me back down. "Press," she demanded.

I got to five reps and hesitated.

"Go for eight," she insisted loudly, and just to show her and Slo I was stronger than they thought, I did them without even grunting. But my pecks were jumping all on their own when I was done.

"That's good," I declared, sitting up and looking for Nor. "Where's North?" I asked, my uneasiness growing.

"She decided to hit the saunas," Robyn said impatiently.

"She hates the saunas," I retorted, standing up.

Slo came over with a jump rope and playfully snapped it at me. "Finish up what you're doing." She began skipping rope with a dexterity that was meant to shame me for wanting to quit.

I gritted my teeth and pressed the weight Robyn had prepared for me, almost giving out on the fifth rep.

"Do it!" Robyn barked. The fleshy part of her thighs was even closer to my face as she crouched ready to take the bar from me should I actually fail. "Shove it up there," she yelled scathingly.

A roar from somewhere down in my belly got the bar up, and that was it, I was through with that exercise.

"Not yet," Robyn growled, and Slo anchored me to the bench with her knee.

"Get off me," I snarled.

"You're not even tired yet," Robyn said, smacking my face to get my attention.

I struck at her, but I couldn't move with Slo's knee in my stomach, so I struck her in the side to make her move, and saw her paw coming at me with frightening clarity. It smashed me across the cheek so I saw stars and wanted, for one long hateful moment, to cry.

"You goddammed Fucker!" I screamed.

She grabbed me by the throat. "I thought you wanted to work out," she drawled, and shoved me back onto the bench.

I snatched up the bar and pumped it three times.

Robyn grunted her approval and upped the weight. Suddenly, the fight went out of me; I knew I couldn't even get the bar up once. Robyn, after shouting at me, had to take it. I was panting and shaking.

"Try it again," Robyn insisted.

"No." They didn't know anything about me and my work-out, and I wanted them to fuck off and leave me alone.

"Like Robyn says, you're a natural wonder," Slo said, shoving her face right into mine. "But you don't know how to take it, and that's no good. If you want to work for us, shape up and get that barbell over your head!"

"Go to hell!" I shouted, and was half-way across the room when I was felled by a blow to my back. I scrambled up, grabbed a wooden exercise bar and held it out in front of me. Slo retrieved the medicine ball she'd thrown, then stood close by, tossing it up and down.

"Let's get some leg work in, ok?" she asked as if we were on friendly terms. "Some of the Gals you'll be Topping are extra special BIG. You're not quite beefy enough to handle them yet."

I swung the bar at her, but she stepped to the side and heaved the medicine ball at my midriff. When I tried to get out of the way, she knocked the bar from my hands and bear-hugged me around the chest. I thought she was going to break my ribs. I heard them crack as she slung me to the side then dragged me towards the mat. It was awful; though I kicked and cursed her, I was ineffectual, and once she hurled me to the mat and nailed my lower back with her knee, I was truly pinned.

"You going to work out for us or not?" she hissed.

I swung my fists backward at her, but the pain she applied to my lower back was more than I could take, and I contemptuously agreed to do some squats.

I was proud of the strength in my legs and nonchalantly pressed everything they demanded of me, then marched over to the leg press machine with a sneer. By the time they had me working my hamstrings, my entire body was jelly-like and slightly euphoric, though I treated Robyn and Slo with heightened disdain, not wanting them to know of my pleasure nor how tired I was; when Robyn praised me, I snorted sarcastically, unimpressed with what she thought.

"You got lots of spunk left in you, Girl."

"I'm not your Girl."

Robyn glared at me, "Get over to the mirror. I want you to work on your biceps."

"You know, I've just about had enough of this. Who do you two think you are? If I'm going to work for you, I want to be treated with some respect."

Slo said, "Hope your girl, North, is having a good time."

"What do you mean?"

Robyn smirked quietly as she handed me a barbell.

"You said yourself she hates saunas. I sent her up to your room with Van."

"You did not!"

"Yes, Ma'm. It'll get her some practice on the other side, too. You know, balance things out a bit"

Furious, I dropped the barbell at Slo's feet, denting the floor as her hand dented my head. I was mad, and flung the bench at her before she'd regained her balance, then got her up side of the head with a weight belt I snatched off the wall.

Robyn grabbed me from behind, and they were all over me, roughing me, shoving me this way, and that, exhausting me more than really hurting me. Finally I just huddled on the floor in a heap.

"Now, " Slo said, panting hard, "finish your work-out."

I nodded dumbly. "What's left?" I asked, miserable about North. Was she really doing it to Van in our room?

Robyn had me do bicep, tricep and wrist curls, several different deltoid exercises, and finally sit-ups off the end of a bench. She sat on my feet and wrapped her arms around my folded up knees. I was so pumped full of clean blood I was floating and nearly mindless. Even after fifty of the super duper sit-ups, I didn't complain. Robyn wanted me to go for a hundred, and lightly slapped my belly to loosen me up. I managed it, but I don't know how. Vaguely, I even liked Robyn and Slo, maybe I was even crying as I completed the last set. I didn't care.

"You'll do," Slo said softly as she guided me gently to the floor and expertly kneaded the soreness from my flesh.

I listened to them breathing somewhere above me, then to their footsteps, receding. The lights clicked off. Hazily, I lifted my head. Were they really, truly gone? The door creaked open again, and I groaned.

"Teddy?"

It was North. I struggled to sit up. "I'm over here," I muttered.

The lights came back on, making me blink. Squatting alongside me, North hesitantly stroked my hair off my forehead, and I let her though it cost me in humiliation to have her see me in such a state. She seemed pleased that I had let her touch me and tenderly stroked my cheek.

"What are you doing in the dark?" she wanted to know.

I winced when she touched the bruise left by Slo's hand.

"Where've you been?" I asked plaintively, angrily shifting away from her.

"Waiting for you."

I pretended I was wiping sweat off my face. "You look great," I mumbled. Her blond hair was ruffled, as if she'd been taking a nap. I quivered under the warmth of her hand, but could not relent to kindness, and rallied my second wind.

"Come here," I said, and took her into my arms. I kissed her neck and eyelids, kissed her mouth as I firmly laid her down on the mat. Propped above her on trembling arms, I exalted in my position; I meant to have her, and she was willing. I was rough because I was eager, turning her over and getting her shorts down over her ass. I felt shudders go through her when I dipped my tongue into her crack and licked the groove a couple of times before I went directly to the hole. I rimmed it, I forced my way in, withdrew, buried my face and played my fingers into her cunt. I was nearly desperate with wanting her to give way beneath me. I wanted to hear her begging me for more.

"Yeah, Baby, you're coming with me," I crooned.

"What do you want me to do, Teddy?" North panted, straining backwards into my face, onto my hand that insisted her cunt stretch wider.

"Yeah, let me in," I cried out. "My whole fist this time!" Inserting another finger, I rode her willingly towards the vision.

The Fey

In Stanley Park, there's a place for women only. Some call it The Fey. Last summer I went there to Pose, usually late in the evening, dressed all in leather. I generally lounged in the lowest crotch of one tree in particular, and played with the tongs of my whip. Of the women that came by, some liked it in their mouths, others how it was meant to be, on their skin. One woman wanted nothing more than to lick my leather thighs; someone else begged me to tie her to a tree, then wait for a crowd to gather before I had my way.

This summer I decided I'd try it as a Walker. My first time I was nervous, and walked through the hetero part of the park without noticing anyone. When I came to the North path, I stopped to smooth my hair and tie my shoelace, then loped across a small meadow, jumped a minute stream, and charged up a short grassy hill, pausing to catch my breath at the top. Below me, there was a lush, tangled woods: The Fey. Glancing around, I hurriedly descended the hill, ducked under a protective tree limb, and entered that magical place.

I'd heard of a Band that guarded the magical parameters, but I'd never seen them. I'd also heard that some few years back, a crone had spell bound the small territory so that no man could enter, even if he was able to perceive the place. I breathed in the pine scent and started walking the main path. Almost directly, I came upon Van. She considered herself the Welcomer, liked to clean every woman's cunt before she continued on her way. The year before, being a Poser, I knew Van because every woman I took had gone through Van, first. Now, I was about to experience her expert tongue. She massaged my tense shoulders, my lower back, then made me jump when she caressed my ass.

"Let me," she encouraged, kneading the stress from my buttocks.

It did feel good. Her hands seemed to understand every knot in me. I just couldn't quite get the hang of letting her do it, though. I wanted to take over, start rubbing her in preparation for spreading her legs and going inside. She was at my fly, stroking it as if she'd found more tension; unbuttoned it with such sincere desire to please me that I gulped down the last of my nervousness and let her have her way. She held me by the hips as she lapped and delicately chewed my juices.

"Don't want you to come, now," she burbled into my wet. "Just getting you ready for your big night."

Then she scented my inner thighs with some kind of powder before buttoning me back up, tucking my shirt and receiving me with one long wonderful kiss. I was ready to start walking.

I stepped off along the path, possibly a little wide-eyed, and suffered my first disappointment; the Big Rock was empty. I'd posed there once, right up on top, and had had a great time enticing women, yet always remaining just out of reach. I almost passed on by, but a flash of color poking up above Big Rock made me look again. I thought it was a bird, but when I saw it again, realized it was a plume of feathers, and went at the sloping stone with confidence and a good fast run. The gray green lichen gave away beneath my scrabbling fingers, however, and I slid back to the ground. I well knew I couldn't get around the sides of the rock; the trees were too dense. As I prepared for another attempt, I heard a whimsical piping that made its way into my brain and took over. Immediately I felt emboldened, light and lustful, and easily scaled the rock, straddling it's familiar solid ridge. On the other side the trees had left a nook where a woman sat on a bright colored blanket, playing her flute. She was naked except for a red strip of cloth around her left bicep, and a feather headdress on her head. Her dreadlocks fell wild and ropy to her shoulders, and when she bent her head back to look at me, her smile was full of deep purpley lips and very white teeth. Returning to her silver flute, she played for all she was worth and slowly shifted her legs so I could see the wet folds of her labia.

I looked for a way down. She flicked encouragement at me with her strong, brown eyes, a look that got me turned around and gave me the impetus to let go; I landed with a thump between her outstretched legs.

Dark red laughter issued from her lips. "Eat me, Dyke." she crooned, and vigorously renewed her song. I went face down into her brown pink folds as if my thirst was the only thing that mattered. I couldn't understand how I'd scaled the rock so easily, when many women had pined after my display, but couldn't get higher than the toe of my boot, but, with the woman's music in my head, her thighs closing about me like a dark cave, I devoured her cunt without further thought.

Afterwards, lightly dizzy, I saluted her by kissing her hand, and mounted the rock, seemingly with the help of her fluted sound. I paused at the top to survey the world below, then slid back down with my own cunt warmed and ready for some action.

A little further along the path, a woman sat by a basket of oranges. Three women kneeled expectantly in front of her. I was curious, and edged a little closer. The small, freckled woman took an orange from the basket, bit into the rind, then deftly hooked a finger under the flap of skin and smoothly laid it open. Pale orange drops glistened on her large veined, wonderful hands; her eyes were infinitely loving. Juice ran down her arms as she tore the orange globe open with narrow teeth. The three women shifted closer to the pungency. I found I was on my knees, too, waiting, straining, hoping we'd be offered some of the fruit from those sculptured hands. When she held them out, we fell to licking and gulping, nudging each other out of the way as we took everything she fed us. We cleaned up every bit of pulp left on her skin, and nosed around for more; "Give us a nipple," we pleaded, pawing at her dress, but she shook us from her with tender care and invited us to mosey along.

I was sticky and crashed through some underbrush to wash myself in the mere trickle of a stream. While my hands and face dried, I hunkered down and sorted out my thoughts. I'd had fun so far, but as a Walker wasn't I supposed to get fucked? I felt anxious, then angry; stood up to ease my teased cunt, then vowed to keep Walking until I got what I wanted, and with purposeful stride, returned to the path. I was busily scanning a clump of trees to my right, and collided with a bruising rush of muscle. My ready retort faded under the bold gaze of the lean woman whose hand steadied me. Her eyes slid to my crotch.

"You ran into me," she said playfully, clearly liking what she saw.

I touched her shoulder, then the entire length of her arm, and ended up by holding her hand. She came to me, smelling of strength, and cupped me where I was heavy and damp. I stiffened expectantly against her.

"It's a hot evening, isn't it?" she whispered into my ear. Just as she began pressing me tightly there was a high, two-tone blast of a whistle. It snapped her head up. Involuntarily I looped my arms around her neck, wanting her back, but she moved away from me, true regret on her face.

"Sorry, Baby," she moaned. "Later, ok?"

I felt hot all over as if there was something wrong with me. The sounds of my warrior's frantic flight receded into nothingness. A lady dressed all in lavender called to me with waving scarves to join her as I stumbled by. Further on I witnessed two women urging another Walker into their midst. She groaned and scratched at her clothes, but the two Posers slapped her efforts into obedience. She gladly bore first one woman's weight, then the other's, then both at once as she went under, whispering madly, "Don't stop, don't stop!" I wanted to jump on top, too. Just listening to her brought my blood to a healthy boil. It was better as a Poser, I thought, and headed spiritedly down the path for my favorite, and lucky, tree.

When I got there, I leapt up and grabbed hold of the first, thick branch. A scratchy yarling sound, much like a wildcat, startled me, and I let go. I looked up into the approaching night. A sickle moon hung between two branches. I peered harder and finally located a woman shape near the top of the tree, flattened along a branch. She barked and chattered then fell silent.

I answered awkwardly with a poor imitation, rousing her delight and a monkey-like behavior; murmuring little soft grunts, she started down towards me, stopped about half way and scooped the air with urgent gestures for me to meet her and play.

I climbed beyond the first crotch. She sat above me, criss-crossed all over with ragged strips of tanned rawhide, her legs swinging. As I moved higher, she sidled towards the top, calling me on with a low purring that whetted my hunger for the chase. I climbed faster, up where the limbs got smaller and the tree's rhythmical motion was intoxicating. Finally she had to stop. I wedged myself just below her, wrapped my legs around the trunk, and reached for her feet. Her achilles tendons flexed out of my range. Maneuvering into an upright position, securing a place for both feet and hugging the central trunk, I brought my face up to the same level as her stomach. There were strands of something tinkly woven into her hair. She tugged at my tee shirt, helped me take it off, then took a small vial from a pouch tied to her waist, and anointed me with her scent. When she kissed me, it was sweetly; then she dropped lower, pulled at me so my bare belly scraped on the bark, and let me into her mouth.

Beneath her skin her muscles lifted and tensed as she squirmed closer to my warmth. Excited to command her, I bit her lip; released her and, taking her shapely head between my hands, was about to kiss her again with bruising force, when she slipped my grasp. Laughing, she began a swift descent.

Hurriedly stuffing my shirt into my back pocket, I followed the slope of her back, the bounding curves of her ass, and caught her wrist about half way down. We stood on the same sturdy branch, panting softly, barely touching. I tasted her blood oozing from a scratch on her arm, twirled her cunt hair into ringlets with two fingers that happened upon her slipperiness, causing our aura to crackle. Lifting my hand to her mouth, she cleaned my thumb with urgent thoroughness before presenting it to the opening of her cunt and interlocking her hands around a branch above her. With bark biting my shoulder, I went directly inside; she ballooned up larger than my thumb.

"Clean me," I insisted, giving over my hand as I pressed her with the rhythm of my hips.

Tucking her knee behind one of mine for stability, she slurped dirt and her own juice until I was clean enough for reentry; home I went into her hot flesh, wide heated balloon, entrance to her womb.

"Witch me!" she sobbed, keeping me steady in and out to the point where she gushed out all over my hand and I had reached a momentary end to my stamina.

I would have rested in the warm coming night until ready to go again, but her thankful hands pressing my back also let me know I should leave. Our goodbye was one mingled happy sigh; I jumped from the lowest branch to the ground, put on my tee shirt, stretched, and headed for home. It was close to dark, though the moon cut pathways and came slanting down through the trees, providing ample light to see my way. I thought I heard something move behind me and turned to investigate. No one was there. I fancied I heard the clank of metal against metal, but then wasn't sure, and chided myself for being frightened of a pine bough creaking. I made myself walk rather than run, though I prickled all over with muted terror. Suddenly, out of nowhere, I was shoved hard enough to make me sprawl. When I lifted my head up off the ground, I saw leather hi-tops of all colors surrounding me in a tight circle.

A hand offered to help me up. I took it and came face to face with the woman who'd left me, earlier. Disgruntled, I brushed off my jeans, and would have pushed by the woman standing next to me, except for the others hemming me in.

"Hello again."

I nodded perfunctorily.

"Sorry about leaving you like that. When The Pack calls, you have to go," she whispered meaningfully, indicating the other women with a slight tilt of her head. Except for her, they all had fat tire bicycles, denim vests decorated with silver studs, and two nasty looking bamboo sticks shoved through their belts.

Someone hissed and the place was lit by a powerful beam. The one who clipped the flashlight to her vest and hauled it up a nearby tree was short and stolid. She lashed the light to a branch so the beam held me in its spot. I shifted out of it, but the tall one seized my arm and brought me back in.

"They call me Jeb."

She seemed a little nervous. I shook her hand off. "Hey, later, ok? I'm not up for a group scene right now."

Behind me, a commanding grunt cut me off. I glanced around uncertainly as the women drew their sticks and held them aloft, as if ready to strike.

"Who are they?" I stepped closer to Jeb for protection.

They clacked their sticks together and shuffled counterclockwise inside the outer ring formed by their bicycles.

"What is this?"

Jeb handed me a small pot of something red and oily. "You must paint a stripe under each of their eyes, and one line down the middle of their chin," she told me.

It seemed very important to her that I should do it; besides, her little finger had surreptitiously caressed mine when she handed me the pot, and I couldn't help wonder what her whole hand would feel like inside my pants. I dipped my forefinger into the paint and approached the woman most directly in front of me. She yipped loudly and the tempo of the dance, if that was what it was, changed. I slabbed a smear of red beneath her eyes. She didn't once betray an awareness of me. I put a stripe on her chin. They beat their sticks faster as I painted in a clockwise direction. It took me a little while, but not once did I witness fatigue in their faces, nor did any of their arms tremble with the effort of keeping those sticks above their head and constantly moving. When I finished I paused to appreciate my handiwork, then turned proudly to find Jeb kneeling in the center of the circle dressed only in cut off jeans. She indicated I should do her face. With more care than I'd used thus far, I put red beneath her eyes, and was about to put the one on her chin when she shook her head no.

"Later," she said, causing me a chill.

The clacking changed rhythm. The women pounded their sticks on the ground in between striking those of the women next to them; the tempo picked up; it was louder, much more insistent, and the direction of the dance reversed. Jeb put her hands on my shoulders. I sensed the women were closing in on us while the bikes held the outer circle secure, and kept trying to look around as if that would maintain my bearings. However, Jeb's gaze possessed my will, and I shakily looked in while the clacking sticks and leather hi-tops tightened the weave until even my breath was part of it.

"Now we're going all the way, eh, Baby?" Jeb squinted her eyes at me to make me stay, and knelt down to untie my tennies. On her way back up, she undid my jeans. She wanted all of it off. Everyone started singing as I fumbled to comply. Standing naked before Jeb, I was tempted to cover my cunt. Her eyes looked red because of the paint. Then she touched me, brushed me all over with her hands, and I shivered; not because I was cold, but because I wanted to trust her.

Several women picked me up and laid me over backwards, across a table of strong backs. Jeb, lit from behind, hovered above me, a body of shadows descending.

I think there were sticks on us, ever so lightly beating a rhythm to the rhythm of her hands in and out of me. Maybe it was rain on our skin, or maybe it was all a dream in which Jeb received her bicycle and studded vest after I painted the stripe on her chin. Later, when I opened my eyes and found myself propped against a tree on the very edge of The Fey, I wasn't sure. I got myself upright with the help of a tree branch, then brought my hand up close to my face; there was a minute dab of red under the fingernail.

A Thursday Night Gathering

K.C. polished her boots. Across town, Flynn oiled her new knife sheath. Regina Laba's lover had been clingy all day and didn't want Regina to go to the meeting advertised in the personal section of The Seattle Gay News: "Sex Worship on Thursday Nights, eight o'clock." There was an address, and in lower case letters, "for women only".

Van was in town for the weekend and thought Sex Worship sounded like fun. Molly sat alone at her dining room table eating cold pizza. At first she was inclined to skim right over the article, but in the course of reading the rest of the paper (she read the personals first), her eyes returned to it several times.

Whit hoped the meeting would be therapeutic.

The gathering was held in a small hall, once a church, painted white on the outside. K.C. shoved the door open and walked in, fingering the soft leather pouch hanging from her belt. A woman was standing on a small podium, five women on folding chairs in front of her, and behind, candles burning on a table made into an altar of sorts.

"Shall we come together?" the woman proclaimed loudly, after she'd waited for K.C. to move a chair out of the prearranged semicircle and sit down. "My name is Jade. I'm here tonight to worship SEX." She paused to pass her eyes over each woman before her; her smile radiated welcome, warmth and possible invitation down upon her audience. "Isn't sex greater than we are? Shouldn't we bow down before it?"

Dressed in her blue blazer with the gold emblem on the breast, and khaki slacks, Molly sat very erect, as if she'd pressed herself as well as her clothes.

K.C. underwent an electric whirring in her blood. It'd begun first thing she'd stepped through the door and set her eyes on Jade; a sensation she'd heard about, heart strings going zing!, but not something she'd ever taken seriously. She slouched in her chair as if she could get away from the unfamiliar churning in her system, the terrifying bubbles of longing and want that threatened to burst free and change her forever.

Van squirmed happily on the edge of her chair. She agreed with Jade; sex was what mattered the most to her, too. She thought of it as the art of smouldering and exploding. She liked the slow, tortuous explosions best; more like implosions of heat that took her out of her body into past life experiences. When she came back, it was always with renewed love for life, as well as a curbed impatience for more.

"We're here together in the name of SEX!" Jade had fine, strong arms that she liked to fling about, and large shapely hands that beat lightly upon her chest, or rested provocatively on her hips. Her eyes were the vivid color of her name; they snapped and sparkled beneath black brows and thick black hair that seemed almost to foam with life.

Whit felt faintly embarrassed; she hadn't expected such fervency. The woman next to her played with a voluminous gauzy scarf of a soft lavender hue. Regina Laba, always alert for performance tips, eyed Jade critically through the scarf she gently floated about, stirring her scent into the air. She noticed the woman with the bone-handled knife at her belt sniffing and smelling the wafted scent with slit-eyed pleasure. She was almost drooling, Regina Laba noted, and playfully laid the gauzy material over her black heels with the tiny silver toe caps, covering her legs at the same time, then twitching the scarf off one seductive inch at a time. Flynn palmed the handle of her knife as she envisioned slitting Jade's stockings; she actually thirsted to lick Jade's plump calves, to gently gnaw and knead the firm, rounded muscles with her teeth and tongue.

"Let's go around and tell each other who we are." Jade leaned forward so the tops of her breasts were visible to them all. Molly uncrossed her legs, recrossed them, different leg on top. Her pale eyes appeared feverish behind her glasses, and she kept her hands tightly folded in her lap. "I'm going to put our names on the altar of SEX!" Jade swiveled around and patted the table with its black cloth and bright burning candles, a movement that stretched her tight skirt even tighter across her buttocks. Flynn wanted to cut the skirt off, too.

"Later we'll tell each other what we've done and exalt in our glorious deeds!" The echo of her voice faded as she implored them with outstretched hands, light winking off her ornate rings.

"I'm Van," Van said, rising from her chair and presenting herself to each woman in turn by going down on one knee and lightly kissing a hem or a crease of fabric, and with such willing readiness that Jade feared the meeting would be out of her hands right then and there.

"Van," she acknowledged with sever tone, implying Van should sit down, and shifted her questioning gaze to the next woman.

Regina paused theatrically, waved her scarf as her primary introduction, unveiled her face, gently tossed her auburn curls off her face and murmured huskily, "Regina Laba."

A performer, Jade thought. She smiled politely and moved on.

"Flynn." Flynn tweaked the bill of her old leather cap.

"Flynn." Jade mouthed the name slowly as she wrote it down. Flynn lusted after Jade's long, white throat.

"My name is Molly," Molly stated loudly, briskly, her clenched hands digging into her lap, then passed the focus on to Whit who was expecting it to go the other way, towards the tall, angry looking woman to Molly's left.

"Whit," she blurted all in a rush, almost choking on the word.

"I'm sorry, we didn't hear you," Jade responded, pen poised above the next slip of paper.

"Whit, uh, Whitsun."

Jade liked Whit's large, gentle eyes in her otherwise inscrutable though beautiful face, and the evident power of her muscles. "That's an interesting name." Gripping the edge of her podium, Jade leaned forward, solely for Whit's benefit, and smiled. Her figure was full and firm, so very ripe beneath the loose cotton blouse and the tight black skirt. Whit bolted inward, startled by Jade's forward approach, incapable even of knowing what she felt in return, though her exterior became all the more handsome, as if she were throwing everyone off the track of her timidity. Jade preened at the altar of Whit's impenetrable, mask-like beauty, rather Greek in profile, and so long and lean and glowingly healthy of body.

K.C., already struggling with dark green jealousy, a struggle she'd always sworn she'd never engage in, glowered at Jade who reverently inscribed Whit's name on paper and placed it with hope for herself on the altar. She turned around and silently questioned K.C. with a look that was distracted, certainly less personal than the one she'd favored Whit with. K.C. crimped her mouth sullenly and kicked the leg of the chair in front of her.

"Tell us who you are," Jade prompted, fully taking K.C. in for the first time; the heavy muscled limbs, her pulsating, dangerous aura.

"I don't like telling people my name."

"What should we call you then?" Jade replied irritably.

K.C. resented Jade's sneery tone and was of a mind to stomp out.

"Prick?" Flynn whispered jokingly, having watched K.C. stroke her soft leather pouch for the past several minutes.

K.C. wrenched around in her chair. There was fighting in her eyes. "Yeah, Fat One," she retorted, looking Flynn up and down.

"Fool, she doesn't want you," Flynn hissed, her hand on her knife butt, in case K.C. didn't understand the friendly advice.

The words pricked K.C.'s hostile overlayer, went directly to her heart, causing it to bleed just a little. "Well, I don't want her either," she muttered with pumped bravado, successfully slathering over the crack in her veneer.

"Tell us who you are! We don't have secrets here." Jade spoke with clean, harsh tones. K.C. bristled under the order; Van studied the supple black boots on Jade's feet, the sharp tack heels of Ms. Laba's shoes, K.C.'s heavy footwear, Whit's and Molly's polished shoes, then Flynn's run down tennies, with rapt longing to lick them all as she eased them off, one foot at a time. "All those toes," she chanted quietly to herself; "All those toes to suck on!"

K.C. actually spat on the floor, then with abrupt contradiction, regretted it and swallowed the lump of defensive anger plaguing her throat. She stopped kicking the chair in front of her, and rode a tight rein on her discomfort, having decided to prove Flynn wrong. "I'm K.C.," she announced gruffly, protectively crossing her arms across her chest.

"Welcome," Jade replied, a little taken aback by the change in the tall, rough-hewn woman whose pupils now glistened with far reaching depths. Admittedly momentarily vulnerable to the gaze, Jade wrapped her hand around her throat, then shook off the sensation of dropping into something over her head, dashed K.C.'s name on the scrap of paper before her and laid it on the alter.

"Welcome to us all!" she rejoiced, lifting her palms to the ceiling. We've come together to worship our SEX. Let us tell each other what we've done!"

Regina laughed out loud and stood right up. "I'll tell you what I've done!" She unwrapped her head and let the scarf float seductively about her bare shoulders as she prepared to tell her tale.

Whit, thoroughly unnerved by the very idea of self revelation, folded a piece of gum into her mouth and chewed it with a circular, grinding motion. She craved a cigarette but didn't want to draw any attention to herself; didn't want to get up and leave for the same reason. So well did she cover her feelings, she looked nothing more than cool, as beautiful as a statue, what with her heart shaped lips and gold-brown skin. Inside, her stomach ate upon itself.

"I met this woman, and I had to have her; I think my lover knows," Regina added, bowing her head unpenitently. "Oh Goddess," she moaned, clasping her hands that she be pitied her unavoidable lapse. "She just looked so damn whippable!"

"Hail The Cry of The Whipper!" Jade cried out ecstatically.

"She has this fine, long back," Regina continued, crossing to Van and caressing Van's back with her scarf. "She wears leather wristlets and anklets, with gold rings braided in." Tapping Van on the shoulder, Regina Laba made it clear she wanted Van to kneel, which she immediately did. "So, I strung her up," Regina recalled in melting tones as she made Van hold her arms in the air as if she'd been strung up. "Do you know what it's like, stringing up a woman to ceiling struts?"

"Uh huh," Flynn growled, her deep-set, werefolk eyes glistening, her fat, sturdy legs planted firmly on the floor.

"Hail the Moment when We String Them Up!" Jade came in with, a little displeased at Regina's lengthy story. Jade wanted short, cathartic confessions, then her fiery response, on and on until they were all swaying and confessing together and singing the praise of their experience.

Molly was faintly frantic, and her jaws hurt from clenching her teeth. Whit finally had to light up a cigarette. The smoke bit her lungs when she expanded her chest and pulled it in: that bite got her breathing again, and that relaxed her belly. Freed of her stomach pain, she felt almost giddy as she pondered Van and wondered how she managed to hold her arms aloft for so long without wavering.

"But, once I got her up, I wanted something else." Regina Laba released Van's arms and turned towards Jade for encouragement to go on.

"Let us hear it, Sister," Jade sang out, beating an accompaniment with her hand on the edge of the podium, thankful to be back on track.

The glorified talk made K.C. want to kick out at someone; she wanted Jade, just the two of them, worshiping SEX by doing it, and tore her fingernail with her teeth.

"I'll tell it how it was," Regina gasped, rocking herself vigorously. "She was strung up, the whip was in my hand, but all I could think about was her piss!" Regina held up her right hand in admission, and before Jade could think of a clarifying response, declared theatrically, "I had to slap her before she'd drink everything I gave her. I really liked slapping her. You know?" she asked pleadingly, swinging about so's to connect with each and every one, stopping at Van whose upturned face triggered a replay. Regina Laba stroked Van's cheek with quivering intent, then swung her small hand with the red nails at Van's face. Flynn flexed forward on her chair. Van made not a sound, though incredibly, she seemed to glow, as with awakened appetite. Regina delighted in the hot sting, the tingle across her palm, the flushed, red mark on Van's skin, and slapped the woman again.

"I've slapped a woman, too!" Molly burst out of her chair, shaking with her need to confess. "You see, I had to whip her! It calms her down!" Molly stood alongside Regina Laba, addressing Jade as if she were the council for her own defense and Jade the Judge. Van struggled with that sliding panic she was so familiar with; the low curdling fear in her belly that there'd be no more. She knew it was her place to wait, however, and she did not plead or beg. "But first, before I whipped her, I slapped her, hard, and she liked it, she whimpered at my feet!" The memory of that moment had burned steadily, like a beacon light, ever since it'd happened, yet this was the first time Molly had uttered it aloud.

"All I could think about was her piss in my mouth. Do you know what that's like?" Regina whispered, clutching Molly's arm and drawing her closer. Molly swallowed loudly and announced with staunch pride,

"I had to do it."

Flynn slid off her chair and crouched low to the floor, absorbing the details of the interchange with an eye for cutting. That scarf, for instance, it hid too much of Ms. Laba's body; and Van was pure misery itself, though she bore it well, and would have welcomed her clothes cut from her. Flynn could see it now, leading the other women one by one to Van, lying naked and innocent on the floor, her plump blushing skin eager for any treatment. It was Jade Flynn truly wanted, though, and she sidled in her direction, right past Whit who'd put her coat back on and was fully prepared to leave.

"I liked it, I liked having her writhing at my feet!" Molly's bony wrists shot out of her ironed pink cuffs as she wildly addressed the ceiling. "Was it so wrong? She liked it, too!" Her arms fell back to her sides, she turned aimlessly from Regina to Jade and back again. Van wished Molly would come to her and have her pleasure there.

"Hail the Sweet Agony of the Lash upon Our Backs!" Jade shouted, furious that her worship was turning into a circus.

"Should I bring them to order?"

Jade started, looked down into Flynn's round face, all the rounder since she'd turned her leather cap backwards. She had her knife in hand, idly polished it as she contemplated the meeting coming apart at its seams.

"It's turning into a free-for-all," Jade complained, her dreams for the evening curling up and going limp.

"Say the word, and I'll bring them to order."

Jade recognized a right-hand woman when she saw one. She laid a thankful, dominant hand on Flynn's fleshy arm, and was surprised at how firm it was. She went red, realizing Flynn knew she'd never really touched a fat woman before, and hadn't known what to expect, except that Flynn might be flabby and possibly a little stinky.

"Oh, Sister, tell it how it is! We want to know what you've done!" Flynn whispered mockingly.

Jade drew back with shattered composure, and caught K.C.'s eye over Flynn's shoulder. K.C.'s fuse was nearly gone from watching the Fat One make up to Jade, then tumble her with some remark that snapped Jade's head back and strained her neck muscles. K.C. stood up, just as Flynn whirled into the middle of the room with a dizzying show of speed and bellowed,

"I'll tell you how it is!" She tossed her knife high above her head, caught it by its blade and flung it at the wall over the altar.

Molly withdrew from Regina's comforting grasp and tugged her cuffs into place. Van prostrated herself and began a long slow slither across the floor so she could lick and honor Flynn's feet.

"Tell us how it is," Jade implored, uncertain why Flynn should forgive her, but willing to accept her graciousness. "Yes, Goddess, tell us how it is," she wailed, sinking back into reverence.

"We are talking about the Gates of Pain!"

"The Gates of Pain!" Jade echoed, pounding her open palm on the podium.

Molly made a move towards her seat, stepping over Van who continued her journey across the floor, acquainting herself with each board. Regina looked miffed; she hadn't finished her story. She shuddered, remembering the hot pee on her face, in her upturned mouth, and how she'd wanted the woman's shit, too; had even squatted and sucked on her ass, sucked and sucked, but nothing came out.

Flynn sprinted around Jade and the altar, plucked her knife from the wall, and returned to the middle of the room, screeching, "Oh, yes, the Gates of Pain!"

"Yes, Sister!"

Flynn cavorted, made a leap sideways, and exclaimed, "I take them there most every time!"

"Tell us what you've done!" Jade cried.

"I took you there," Flynn replied evenly, loud enough for everyone to hear. She pointed her knife right at Jade's heart and advanced. "When you touched my arm you thought it'd be disgusting, painful to your senses, right?" Flynn stopped, her knife two inches from Jade's bosom. "Gate of Pain and it wasn't so bad, even rather pleasurable, no?" Flynn smiled engagingly, with such amiability, Jade was no longer frightened. Van patiently changed her direction and kept on going. "Now, bare your thighs and we will all touch them."

Jade stiffened, she drew herself up haughtily.

"Yes, Sister, let me cut away those stockings, we'll lick away your shame!"

"I'm not ashamed of my thighs!"

"Hallelujah! Gather round!" Flynn lightly pinched Jade's stocking between two fingers, but was prevented from cutting it when Jade jerked out of her grasp. "Flynn, no," she pleaded softly, and Flynn knew, upon looking into Jade's troubled eyes, that Jade simply wasn't ready for that particular Gate of Pain. She retreated, but not before K.C. launched an attack, roaring, "You leave her alone!"

Flynn whirled about and shoved her knife nearly into K.C.'s face. "I've no quarrel with you," she warned, but she looked like she'd have no qualms about finishing K.C. off. Whit stood up, Firefighter responding to a crises.

"Why don't you leave her alone?" K.C. yelled again, then was angry at Jade when she stepped down from her podium and stalked away with a definite show of disgust. She skirted Van, bore down on Regina and Molly who were still reeling from their confessions.

"I guess the meeting is breaking up," Jade told them.

Flynn jabbed playfully at K.C. who growled and stepped back.

Molly, her beacon light burning brighter than ever, wanted nothing more than to get home before Beth so she could shower, freshen herself before they went to bed, and gladly accepted Jade's encouragement to leave. "Well, thank you," she said formally, shook Jade's hand, Regina's, paused uncertainly, then decided not to interfere with the others, and hurried out of the room.

Clutching Jade's arm, Regina said, "It's a wonderful idea, worshipping SEX, I think we should do it every week! You are going to meet next Thursday, aren't you?"

Jade looked around the room, her face tightening at the spectacle of Flynn and K.C., circling each other; "We'll see how it goes," she replied. "I want to, I want us all to 'get down', you know? Together!"

Regina, suddenly gripped by a pang of guilt, covered her face with her scarf. "Maybe I'll bring my lover next week," she murmured. "That would be interesting, don't you think, lovers confessing the pain they'd inflicted upon each other?"

Jade sighed. It sounded too much like therapy. Regina hastily kissed Jade's cheek, and immersed in her lavender cloud, vanished out the door.

Precisely at that moment, Van reached Flynn's feet. Flynn glanced down at the prostrate figure, and in that brief lapse of attention, K.C. sprang for the knife. Flynn blocked the attempt, slashing K.C.'s arm in the process.

"No!" yelled Whit. She was across the room and clutching the wound together even before K.C. quite knew what had happened. "Rip me a piece of your shirt," Whit commanded, without looking at Flynn. "Here, sit down," she insisted, nudging K.C. backwards into a chair as blood seeped out between her fingers and dripped on K.C's jeans and the floor.

Flynn held out a piece of her shirt, and Whit began wrapping the wound. "I'm sorry," Flynn murmured genuinely.

K.C. dazedly watched the bandage soak up her blood.

Knotting the bandage, Whit realized she felt like weeping. "It's not a bad cut," she reassured K.C.

Flynn bent down and petted Van's head. "You want those clothes cut away, don't you?" she crooned, and Van whimpered happily. She knew this was the Goddess who would take her home and undo her until there was nothing more to be done.

Babies whimper like that, Whitsun thought, staring at Van who crawled into Flynn's arms. Bowing her head so her forehead touched the bandage around K.C.'s arm, Whit started crying. She stood up, tears streaming down her face, and blundered into Jade's arms. She laid her head on Jade's bosom, the sweet, full mounds beneath the soft cotton blouse, and allowed Jade to stroke her back.

"Bless you, bless you," Jade murmured in Whit's ear, thanking her for stemming the blood.

Whit smiled weakly, wondrously afloat from the relief tears can bring. "I guess I'd better be heading home," she said, removing herself from Jade's arms and checking K.C. one last time to make sure she wasn't in shock. Flynn pulled Van to her feet and, tipping her cap first at Jade, then at K.C., the two of them followed Whit out the door.

Jade gazed after Whit with mixed relief and disappointment that she hadn't stayed. Maybe she'll come back next week, Jade thought, deciding then and there she'd continue with the meetings. She went about stacking the chairs, chanting under her breath, "Hail, the Meeting Come to Order! Hail us Sweet Sisters of Sex! Hail S/M Glory! Come Together and Confess!"

K.C., her eyes closed, listened to Jade muttering as she moved about clanking the chairs into a stack. "Hail the Cry of The Cut," she mumbled, opening her eyes. The white bandage was becoming quite red. "Hail the Blood that Flows!"

"Are you all right?"

K.C. straightened in her chair. Two twin hoods came down over her eyes, making them somewhat hard, and her mouth twisted carelessly as she said, "Sure, I'm fine." Standing up, however, made her head go weak; or was it Jade?

"The Meeting's over," Jade stated in a tired, flat voice.

"Not for me."

"Everyone's gone."

"Except you and me." K.C.'s chamois pouch swayed at her side as she shifted her weight. She had to keep her arm up or it throbbed.

"Look, I'm not attracted to you," Jade blurted uneasily, avoiding K.C.'s face where the pain her remark roused showed, swift and sure.

K.C. hated herself for the longing she felt; why not just take the Cunt? But her arm held her back. She could see it was still bleeding, and she wanted to give it a chance to heal.

"Hail The Cry of The Rejected!" she said sarcastically. Dammit, why didn't she simply take Jade by the throat and shove her up against the wall?

Jade gestured mockingly at K.C.'s pouch. "Hail The Big Butch!"

K.C. staggered backwards. Her temper flared, hot and roaring in her belly and ears.

"Go home," Jade commanded coldly.

K.C. fought furious battle within herself trying to decide what to do; she felt drunk with the unbearable loss of control, but no matter how hard she whipped herself from within, she knew she was going soft and willing.

"I worship you," K.C. said, lightly placing her hand on Jade's skirt, over her mound. "Hail Ms. Jade and K.C. making it Together!"

Reeling under the spiraling shock of a warm, questioning hand on her cunt, Jade fell forward into it before she caught herself and pulled back.

"No secrets," K.C. reminded her. "Hail the worship of Ms. Jade. Let's put it on the altar!"

Jade felt, rather than witnessed, the hand closing on her hem, slowly dragging her skirt up over her thighs. K.C. hesitated, then lifted it higher.

"Alright, I have wanted you," Jade admitted, her breath raspy, sounding odd to her own ears.

K.C. tenderly guided Jade to the altar, her wounded arm across Jade's shoulders.

Jade laughed then, fingering the long object in K.C.'s pouch as she swept all but hers and K.C.'s printed name off the altar. "Use it on me," she whispered, licking the smell of leather off her fingers.

"Hail the Holy Request!" K.C. parted Jade's legs and pressed her mouth to the damp crotch of the the panty hose covering Jade's lower half. "Hail the Lust of one Woman for Another!"

Jade lifted her hips and peeled away the black hose; held out one shapely leg, and the other, for K.C. to undress, then permitted K.C. to kiss her knobby toes, her calves, but when K.C. reached her thighs, Jade pressed her cunt pleadingly and with outright demand, against K.C.'s crotch. K.C. understood that signal, and blew out all but three candles, put them on the floor, and eased Jade up on the table. Jade welcomed K.C.'s weight on top of her, rubbed her breasts against K.C.'s chest, and locked her legs around K.C.'s waist as they joined together with each thrust.

Make Me Listen

Hurt Me

"Hurt me," I whispered that night, in the pale light of the street lamp coming into her room. I wanted something exquisite: her command. I had crouched over her, doglike, wolf eyes, male, womanskin, then pinned her to the bed with my cunt. My hand went in. I was strong, sweat and fury muscle, locked her hands above her head with one grip. She wanted to be my whore. Dignified student losing face, head tossing side to side, debauched by her ravisher.

"You'd goddam well better love me!" she cried, stricken with new glory, her cunt deeper than she'd ever known.

I did love her. She was everything I wanted to be. And I, fierce, lean Butch, watching her, also wanted to yield. I thought that was what I offered when I said, "Hurt me." I wanted she should pin me open with desire.

She hurt me, but not that night. She said she didn't know how, and proved she did later on, and later yet, and for years, more than I could ever ask for. I did ask for it, but I had thought it would be in bed, with whips and calculated slaps. I'd hoped for her in heels insisting I lick them. I'd thought I'd be tied down and measured by my resistance. I thought I'd learn to spread my legs as wide as she did.

My whore. My female companion, my lady in her pearls and silk and scented bra. I had her, once, because I could take her to the ground with my cunt. I remember how she moaned, her throat gaping open for me, and the willing declaration of her averted face and thighs angled outward as we'd go at it, up against the walls in our haste to get beyond the clothes.

"Hurt me," I whispered our first night. I didn't know what I was in for. I signed myself away; she became Mistress, more than any Butch could want, except it took place outside of bed. The shackles were unrelenting as steel, but I couldn't see them, and the whips were not made of leather. My resistance was measured; I fought back, refused to yield. "Buckle me to my knees," I dared, and she did.

It was the sight of her back, retreating, that got me crying; those prideful shoulders, and the backs of her arms, sleeves pushed up to the elbows, walking the other way.

"Hurt me," I whispered long ago.

"You'd goddam well better love me," she cried out that same night after I'd moored her relentlessly to the bed with my cunt, and showed her the backside, heady side, of my command.

On My Knees

She kept me on my knees a long time. I liked it that way, watching her dress. First she took a bath in scented water. I washed her back, and when she was through bathing, dried her feet, thoroughly eager to please, making little clucking noises in the back of my throat over the condition of her toes, damaged by hundreds of too-tight beautiful shoes.

Her underwear was white. Her bra made of silk. When she reached around behind herself to do it up, her pectorals bulged slightly. I pleaded with her to let me help, but she liked to tease me. She liked me to think I'd never get what I wanted. My asking only brought that superior, knowing smile to her lips all the more. I remained silent, powerless to look away as she put her foot up on a chair, wiggled her toes into her nylon stocking and slowly worked it up over her leg. She talked to me while I squirmed. The black nylon covered up her calves, knees, inched up over her long thighs; I tried to avert my eyes. My palms were sweating. I wanted her and watched as she covered up her underwear with one last, firm tug.

Once she'd smoothed her leather skirt down over her ass, she turned around and asked if I would do up the few buttons. I lingered over the task as long as I possibly could, and checked myself from sliding my cheek up her backbone, then reaching up to cup the weight of her breasts. I just wanted to hold them. She put on her shirt. It was white and crisp. She did up the front, then wrapped a wide black leather belt about her waist. Standing directly in front of me, she teased my cheeks and mouth with the pointed ends.

Leather in my mouth. Her leather, wet and stinging, across a cheek. I clung to her wide, sturdy hips and prayed it would go on. I saw her consider the bedroom, and began kissing her through her clothes. She bent my head back and slapped me hard, reminding me she was in control and would make the decisions. We both knew, the way our breath came ragged and hot into out throats, that we liked it. My muscles coiled on the floor at her feet.

"Will you put my shoes on?" she asked.

I hurried to fetch her black heels. I'd polished them earlier, and when she wasn't looking, had slid each spike into my mouth and out. Apparently she had seen me because she made me do it again. Then she took the slim shoe and fucked my mouth with the spike until I was dizzy and she panting, and it was time for me to put it on her foot.

"I have some people coming over," she told me.

I tried to hide my disappointment, the rush of jealousy that almost overtook me. People coming over! And me in that state, wanting her, teased out of all proportion. I knew it wouldn't do any good to protest. She didn't like it when I made demands.

I watched from a corner of the room as she greeted her friends at the door. They were mostly women, a few men. Everyone was well dressed, no one on their knees, though each of them sidled up to her charm as if bowing, hoping to excite her favor. I was collared, made to heel, my leash in her hand or looped through her belt when she got to talking. She used her magnificent hands to help shape what she had to say. I didn't like how the men moved in on her, their eyes unmistakably lustful. Her laugh was loud and never failed to race deliciously up my spine, but when she boldly gave it over to those men, with faint sarcasm, letting her eyes drift down the front of their pants, I tugged hard at my leash. That's how she looked at me, sometimes, times when we were alone and I had at her any way I pleased. I glared and snarled at the men until they moved on. I didn't mind the women crowding around her half as much. Mostly they wanted to be next to her, to smell her perfume and watch the light catch in her jewels. If they did want more than that, I sat up on my haunches and bared my teeth, making sure they settled for less.

I didn't like crowds. Acting polite tired me out. I wanted to back her up against the wall, tell everyone to go away, and take her without asking. I wanted attention for me. I wanted to be beautiful, too. But, I realized I was becoming unruly. She kept jerking on my leash, hissing under her breath for me to behave.

Finally everyone went home. I was on edge from all my waiting, and dog-like in my lavish attention on her, in hopes that we'd go directly to the bedroom. She was moody and distant. I removed her shoes, rubbed her feet. I listened to her talk, loved the resonant tones of her voice tumbling over me. We drank pale champagne, very dry, very cold, touching the rims of our crystal together. I lit candles for the occasion. She complained about my behavior at her party.

"You were rude, weren't you?" she asked, rising from her chair with a flourish, crossing the room in that inimitable stride of hers to fetch her whip.

I started to tremble.

"You didn't say anything," she exclaimed, striking me. "It's rude to act so glum." The words penetrated my skull as the hoped-for lash sliced through my cells. Then, for one long moment, I wanted to rebel. I felt defensive.

She was irate, whirling whip and words, forcing me lower than my knees. Her nipples stood erect through silk and cotton, her pelvis was thrust forward, her breasts swelling to voluptuousness beneath her blouse. I loved her strong hands bringing the lash to my back, and loved her face, especially since I knew, once she was through with her tirade, she'd soften, ready for me to have my way.

Later that night, still on my knees, but in the luxury of her bed, I had her crouch, face against the pillow, ass high in the air. It was very dark. No one could see. Just between her and I, she was my whore. The decadent lady gone to the streets.

75

"I want it, your dildo," she moaned.

I had anticipated this. The dildo was by the bed. I moistened the tip with my lips and laid it on the soft inner part of her thigh. Enough to drive her crazy, moaning and calling out my name, reaching back with her hand to spread her labia. It was easy, sliding the dildo and part of my hand inside her. She was wet and huge and gaping open for penetration. She wasn't ready to have me inside her ass, though, except for my tongue, as far as it could reach. Her elegant hands twisted about the bed posts while I rimmed her, licked and sucked, riding each thrust and undulation with an intensity that outlasted her stamina.

She slept. I was tethered to her side, and stroked her deeper into the dream state, wishing she wouldn't leave me quite so quickly. In the dark I listened to her breathe, to a small snore rattling each exhale. There was no sleep for me. I wanted endearments and the skin of her hands on my hide. My back burned, scored by her nails. I liked being marked by her, and comforted myself for awhile, pleasuring in the pain. But the night seemed darker than any other I'd known. I chaffed against my tether. I wanted her to wake up, and fidgeted until finally she did.

I was frightened by the sounds of anger bubbling from my lips. "Something's wrong," I kept saying.

"What?" she wanted to know, slipping back into sleep.

"Don't leave me," I pleaded, desperately wanting her to hold me.

But sleep wasn't something she could hold off, I knew that. It took her as easily as I did. I worked at my tether and couldn't get it undone. And if I did, where would I go? Where could I ever find anyone as essential to me as she was? Besides, she had a gun.

Sometimes she'd press it up next to my head. Of course I'd be on my knees, trembling, having some difficulty swallowing. I'd keep hoping she'd put it inside of me. I didn't know what I wanted. Maybe to stand up and have her blow my brains out. She'd stroke my hair. I was allowed to feel her legs and kiss her hem. With a gun to my head, a gun oiled in her perfume and shiny black. She'd bend down so I could see the tops of her breasts, gorgeous swells trimmed in lace. I'd be breathing so hard, anxious tog know she wasn't just teasing me, dripping and foolish on the hard wood floor at her feet. She even cocked the gun, once. I thought it a delicious sound. She kissed me, the muzzle cold against the back of my head. She was a Goddess swaying above me, jiggling a handful of ammunition, tilting back her head to laugh when she saw fear in my eyes. By then my knees hurt. My legs were starting to go numb, and I shook all over; from fatigue, delirious anticipation or absolute terror, I didn't know.

"When are you going to let me up?" I whispered, pressing my face to her hidden cunt. I peered up at her, started to rise. "When," I said a little louder, and ended up by yelling, "When are you going to let me up?"

That smile of hers, lovely and perfect, thrilled me anew. I knew what was coming, our cycle never varied. My punishment, then, in the dark, I could have my way.

Alley of Her Throat

She pressed the point of her knife against my throat, into the soft hollow where the jugular throbs.

"Unbutton your shirt," she said.

I wanted her close but she kept me at bay, stretching the elasticity of my neck to the cutting point.

"Your shirt," she repeated softly.

Her voice, the way she leaned on me with her eyes made me fumble. I undid the first button. She wanted more. She didn't say please, but slid that gleaming knife tip down along the path of my opened shirt, leaving a puckered trail of blood. When the fourth button was undone, her blade scratched the tender casing of my organs. I was frightened to breathe for fear the rising of my belly might cause me to die. Her blade pressing on me like that. I pleaded with her, wanting to know what she meant to do.

"All the way," she insisted, meaning for me to finish with my shirt.

The puckers of blood ran one into the other, and when they swerved in their downward slant, the white cotton was stained. Her hand held the knife without wavering. I loved her large hands, the one promising to slice open my belly if I didn't undo my jeans. She stood so close it seemed I should be able to have her.

"Unbutton them," she insisted.

I balked. I couldn't have her cutting me up down there. I thought it time she let me lick my own blood off her knife. I wanted to remove her silk blouse slow, slower than that. My hands anticipated the wonderful weight of her breasts, my fingers craved to ease the straps of her bra off her shoulders.

"Your pants," she gasped in a voice strange to me. One rough and graveled by some intensity I didn't know.

"Please kiss me," I begged, thinking this would give me the courage to go on.

"No!" she shouted. "Undo your pants!"

Five buttons shoved through their stiff denim holes. I stood before her, her knife's bloodline suspended where my pubic hair begins. I was afraid to touch her, and closed my eyes, hoping I would crave her less if I couldn't see. But there was the excitement of her perfume, the small sounds of her breath, then a sharp coldness sliding lower.

"Go ahead, do me in!" I cried out with a passion for her metal twisting in my guts without relent.

The knife fell to the floor. Her leather skirt creaked. My startled, opened eyes witnessed her descent. Quivering, on her knees, she took hold of my hips and pulled me to her. Looking down on her, it seemed the bloodline disappeared into her face, and, astonished that I was alive in her mouth, closer than a blade, I stretched back into myself under the stroke of her tongue. She opened me up for the pleasure of eating, of listening to my blood roar as it should, in my veins, under the skin her teeth grazed as I came into the alley of her throat.

Beastly

It was raining. Sounded like heavy piss in the gutters. Marlee's heels were gunshot on the pavement as she walked by Dana's apartment window. She wondered if Dana were inside, and if so, who she was making love to. Marlee paused on the corner in the shadow made by a tree and considered knocking on Dana's door. She no longer had her key. Dana had written and asked for it back. Written! when she could just as easily have called. But then, just talking to each other, they'd be wanting to get back together, and Dana had said the week before, "I'm really going to break with you this time!" She was wearing her black jeans and a teeshirt ripped at the shoulder. "This is really it!" she shouted. "Enough of this back and forth stuff! I'm through!"

Marlee decided to walk around the block. It was even darker under the trees on sixteenth; the rain dropped from the leaves and landed with hollow echoes on her umbrella. She knew she was risking finding Dana's motorcycle parked behind the apartment building, and if she did, the sight of it would rip her heart some. Sure enough, it was there. Dark red, gleaming in the rain. Marlee poked her fingers through the wire mesh fence and held on. She wished she had a key. She'd get on and go for a ride. She'd drive it hard down the freeway and let the rain slash her face.

Marlee let go of the fence and told herself to get away from there, but she knew, now that her heart was ripping just a little, she was going to tear it some more, and opened the gate to the back yard. She was careful negotiating the cobbled downslant into the yard, and sorry Dana's windows didn't look down on the scene of her coming to see the familiar beast. Dana would recognize the umbrella, and Marlee could almost hear her laugh, and the loud thuds as she took the stairs two at a time in her eagerness to get outside. Marlee even turned and faced the back door, lit from above by one shaded bulb, as if waiting for it to burst open and Dana to be framed there. Then they'd take each other up into arms, and Dana'd toss the umbrella aside so they could kiss under the rain.

The back doorknob knew no hand, and the windows that did look down upon the scene were tightly drawn with curtains. Marlee heard the beast calling her, begging her for the key with a low, indistinct purr. It was a cold stead to cuddle up to; Marlee patted its high-humped gas tank, and was startled by the resounding clank of her ring on the metal drum. She did it again and again, under the delirious impression that someone would hear and tell Dana her bike was being vandalized. No one seemed to notice. Marlee stopped and stroked the saddle. The rain turned into a drizzle, then into a fine, warm mist that Marlee welcomed with upturned face. It felt like a thousand tiny kisses on her lips and eyelids. She released her umbrella and put it aside on the picnic table. That table! Marlee swooshed leftover rain from its surface with one sweep of her hand. The barbecues they'd had, and once they'd slept under the table, covering it over with a blanket so it was dark and close like a womb.

Now that the rain had stopped, Marlee realized the humidity, and the heavy fragrance of the spring blossoms. The fruit trees whispered scent and ripening; the grass was a tangled lush mat; the oak on the street was bursting, pushing and spreading under a dense blanket of clouds that held the night heat in. The ground even steamed a little. Marlee took off her underpants. They were a white flag in her hand. She dried the red beast with them, with the crotch, already damp from when she stood on the corner in the shadows and hoped Dana would come to the window.

A rustling in the grass made Marlee quiver. She peered into the thick night. It was a cat, long and slinky, with narrowed yellow eyes. Having hoped it'd be Dana playing games, sneaking up, ready to leap with joyous snarls upon her neck and bear her to the ground so's to fuck her on the bruising cobblestone in the steam next to the freshly ploughed vegetable patch, Marlee was severely disappointed. She clucked at the cat, invited it over for a petting, but it flicked its tail and returned to its jungle grass hunting ground.

Marlee took a firm grip on the wide spread handlebars, but could only see Dana's hands, and feel their calm search across the curves of her body. They were never frantic on her, though they could be rough, and were strong enough to snap her. They were animals. They handled her like hounds getting her down to the level of their forceful, lapping tongues. Marlee shook awake from the dream and mounted the steed, bringing leather and labia together. She stood up on the pedals as if going over a jump or lump in the road, and slid back and forth over the seat. There were ridges in the saddle, they tweaked her clit. Back and forth she went, her skirt up over her thighs, and the steam rising up from the damp ground all around.

It was then the moon broke through, and Marlee wanted her nipples tweaked, too. Where was Dana? Why didn't she come out of the square brick building and straddle the saddle behind? Marlee let go the handlebars and plumped her breasts with her own hands, but it just wasn't the same. Accelerating her momentum back and forth across the leather, her labia rolling and sliding, and her clit burgeoning with a wild crazy heat, Marlee howled her ascent. Steam sizzled and flushed in her cheeks, her cunt grew molten inside her, and when she came, she gushed hot liquid. Panting, Marlee sagged against the back rest. Moonlight made jewels of her cum beading up on the highly polished tank. She closed her eyes, imagining Dana walking towards her with one sleeve rolled up, her hand cocked and ready to enter her and bring forth yet deeper howls.

Something pressed her bare knee. Marlee's heart ripped anew

when, certain it WAS Dana, she opened her eyes to a stranger wiping a bit of cum juice off the bike and sucking her finger clean.

"Hmmm," the woman murmured approvingly, then bent her head down and slowly licked up all the juices. She wore a black vest over a white shirt, her fingers were spindly and delicate, surprisingly powerful caressing Marlee's legs upwards from her ankles.

If it couldn't be Dana, she'd have it anyway, Marlee vowed as the stranger pushed her face and head into the cave of Marlee's skirt. Her tongue moved on Marlee differently than Dana's used to. At first Marlee wanted to push the stranger away, but her cunt was Queen and demanded a hand. Marlee gripped the stranger's wrist and placed her hand where her mouth had been. When she surfaced from Marlee's skirts, there was a wet mustache on her upper lip and a tiny wet beard on her chin. Marlee didn't want the stranger to kiss her, but she welcomed the gentle penetration that tipped her back against the padded sissy bar, welcomed a tempo that, if not Dana's, was sufficient to loosen her mind. Marlee became nothing but soft yielding walls gulping upon fingers, and a color nearly the shade of the bike.

The stranger slung her leg over the saddle facing Marlee and showed her what a thin, wiry arm could do. It made Marlee grunt and gurgle low in her throat, and her nipples perk up. The stranger freed them from their restraining blouse, and keeping her weight tipped towards the kick stand so they wouldn't fall over, paid further homage to the Queen. But Marlee didn't howl, though she gushed for the second time, all over the stranger's crotch, staining the light blue cloth. Her breasts ached to be crushed and kneaded; Marlee laid the stranger's hands on them, noticing that the curtains were still tightly drawn and the back door was as locked as ever. The seams of her heart ripped wide as the stranger loved up her breasts and fell to sucking the tender swollen nipples. Marlee cried for the willing mouth on her, unfamiliar lips and no biting teeth; cried for the tension going out of her as the stranger sucked and kneaded her flesh; cried because the back door hadn't opened and Dana hadn't heard her moaning.

A Night At Home

Two women were kissing in the bathroom. Carson happened upon them when she tested the door, found it unlocked, and went right in. One of them was braceleted and necklaced with chains, the other was up on the counter top, her butt half in the sink and half out, giving tongue to her partner whose black leather jacket had a studded butterfly on the back. Carson backed out of the room and returned to her table in the corner. It was Friday night and still early. Carson had been in the bar since five, reading the Gay News and feeling sorry for herself. To make matters worse, everyone else was having a great time.

At the bar three women crowded against each other, laughing uproariously, drinking beer, clinking their glasses and laughing again. The one in the middle was getting the most attention. The outside two fondled her ass from time to time and squeezed her tight between them. She didn't mind, and made the outside two kiss so she could watch, but they ended up kissing her instead. Disheartened into a deeper loneliness by the lascivious display, Carson tried to focus on the paper in front of her. She sipped her sparkly water, then sized up Megan for the hundredth time that night. Carson hardly knew her, but enough to be interested; had been sending psychic messages to her the past couple of hours to at least look up and give romance a chance, but Megan was absorbed in her video game with a hunched over intensity that discouraged Carson from interfering. Sighing hopelessly, she half-heartedly attempted the crossword puzzle just as an athletic bunch burst in through the front door, fresh from a game.

With socks crumpled around their ankles, spirits high and hair moist with sweat, they dominated the room with their odor and rambunctious, self-congratulatory manner. They were loud, they were happy, and claiming two tables, pushed them together. Pitchers of beer were called for, glasses all around, then they toasted themselves with their team cheer. Carson touched her bolo tie to make sure it was still snug up against her collar where it belonged. One of the soccer players in particular drew her eye; she sat slightly apart from the others, and had a raw scrape on one thigh that was still oozing blood. Carson watched her, the indifferent way she had of tossing her hair back; how she played with her glass, then wiped her mouth with the back of her hand when she finished the beer off. Twice she looked right at Carson, drawing Carson to the very edge of her seat, though not intentionally. She was just looking around the room, not taking anything in so much as concentrating on herself as she distractedly gazed about the room. Carson waited for the soccer player's glance to come around again. She felt certain that it would, and basked in a self conscious handsomeness, with her heart banging roughly in her chest, as she waited.

A latecomer entered the bar. She was blonde, not much more than five-foot-two, and went directly to the team table where she was loudly greeted. The aloof one, the one Carson wanted, sat forward in her chair and quickly poured a glass of beer. When she held it out to the newly arrived, there was a look of barely concealed lust between them. Carson felt the magnetism from across the room as a low blow to her self esteem, and though a big woman, she felt she made no impression whatsoever when she walked the length of the room on her way out.

Outside, she paused to collect her senses. The air was sticky, and her sweat smelled sour, yet the night seemed, once again, full of possibilities. She set out, only to come across two women vigorously going at it in the close shadows just half a block from the bar. Snarling silently, Carson crossed the street, went around the corner and turned onto the path taking her through Lashmere Park where the summer heat was less intense. However, there were people whispering under the trees, and the sounds of movement in the bushes, then the sounds of someone coming; Carson fancied it'd be a woman, all alone and looking, but it was two gay guys, one of them in the process of buttoning up his jeans. Carson let them pass and started running. By the time she got home she was panting, her shirt stuck to her, as well as her jeans, but her odor was no longer nervous; it filled her nostrils, clean and strong.

Her apartment was stiflingly hot. She cranked the windows open, drew the curtains, and went into the kitchen where she poured herself a shot of Cuervo Gold. In the bedroom she stood in front of the big round mirror over her bed. Undoing her tie, she tossed it on the dresser, then skinned off her shirt. Balling it up, she chucked it to the back of the closet where the dirty laundry lived. There were three mirrors in her bedroom, all of which flung back at her the image of cowed shoulders and a belly that was much too round. Carson sucked it in, but that only made it look tense. She liked her back, though, long and smooth, sloping nicely into her belted jeans. Carson tipped the golden tequila to her lips as she stepped on the heel of one tennie with the other, thus removing it. When her feet were bare on the carpet, she padded into the bathroom and splashed cold water on her face. It was like swimming, coming up from under, up through the cool depths then bursting free and shaking the clinging drops from hair and eyes. Carson dashed water on her chest, scrubbed at her underarms, then walked into the living room with minute rivulets tickling downwards along her skin.

She chose Ferron for the turntable, and after she'd replenished her fire-water, sat in her big red velour rocking chair to listen. It was lonely music; Carson's spirits were lifted into painful memories of Carol. But that was all over. Going to the window, Carson took hold of the curtain and looked out into the street. No one was there. When the record was through, she turned it over; the music made her ache and want to dance with sad, crazy gyrations. She stepped in front of the mirror over the stereo and saluted herself, then downed the tequila. No lime, no salt to cut the burn. Carson slid her hand down her front, following the path of the fiery fumes; cupped herself and humped her pelvis to the beat of the music. Slowly raising her gaze, she made contact with her own eyes, and watched how she undid her own jeans.

Images of women swirled through her mind. She cupped the balls she imagined she had, and closed her right hand around her thick cock. Shutting her eyes, she let it happen how it came to her; thrusting in and out of the circle made by her fingers, with the muscles in her haunches and legs gloriously powerful; white and hot red heat traveled through her blood into her vortex and brought her coming, gasping, ripped free of everything but that moment of exquisite release.

There was no denying her cunt, then. A candle was nearest at hand. Now she imagined a pack of women wanting to mount her. Stripping off her jeans and getting down on hands and knees, Carson slid the blue candle inside, reaching around to enter herself from behind. Her face was forehead down on the floor, her ass humiliatingly high in the air, but the women wanted it that way. Carson was their slave, she squatted to receive as much of the candle as she could. Even then it hurt. She wasn't used to being entered. She was tight. But the image of the women relentlessly forcing their way in made Carson want it all the more, and she came down harder on the long object within.

When the fucking was over, she went directly to the bedroom for the vibrator. First she lit the anointed candle and put it near the head of the bed. In that light, her stomach looked muscular, and her legs warrioresque rather than lumpish. She laid down on the bed, with her ass once again in the air, and turned the vibrator on. It's gentle hum laid to her clitoris gave off an electric thrill at first too intense, and she had to remove it. Wetting one finger, Carson called the women into the room, envisioning them lining up to fuck her ass. Immediately the vision passed through her and she was open; fumbling under the bed for her dildo, she slicked it up with her tongue, handed it over to the first woman in line, saw the others staring at her with lit up eyes and twitching hands, and buried her cries in the pillow as the entire dildo went right in.

"Let it stay," she moaned when the first woman had fucked her fill. Carson turned the vibrator on again, and used her finger as a buffer between tip and clit. "Crouch over me," she begged. One woman climbed on top, the dildo instantly becoming part of her so she was inside, alive and quivering.

Pinned inside out like that, Carson gave in to the pressure low in her abdomen. It wanted to build, to sweep through her uncontrolled and explode in the end. Several times she lost her seat on the electrical vibrations, the momentum died, but she soon found it again. The woman started riding her ass, and the pressure began detonating in slow gripping circles upwards from her loins. The spasms quickened, she exploded, certain she would come out by the roots; every one of her muscles rallied to the final spurt, and when it was through she collapsed into her own special timelessness under the candle guard flickering overhead.

Let Me Go,
Cum Forever On My Lips

The Rite

Beltane was a wind whipped night. Chicago glittered and shook; signs creaked, stoplights swung dangerously close to snapping free, and the lake was a deep blue black. Hardly anyone was out and about. The night air reigned with the force of galloping horses. Papers and plastic things rattled willy nilly along the streets as the lights in the buildings dipped and shimmered. Beneath the pavement the earth groaned. Trees rushed with the roar of movement, bending nearly to the ground. On the thirteenth floor of one hotel, inside the wind, a writers' conference was underway, having started that very night when Tanya read three stories. Before she read the last one she took several deep breaths, then said, "The Rite to Awaken Desire." Her audience shifted and creaked forward in their chairs. Outside, the wind slammed against the building. Tanya waited for the onslaught to pass, then began reading her story:

"I'll never get it right," Sara complained, shielding her eyes against the lights so she could make out Bonnie's shape in the empty club house.

Bonnie appeared at the edge of the stage, a smile on her face. "You're going to be a hit, Baby."

Sara covered herself with an old robe. "You think so?" she asked uncertainly. "Maybe we should go over it one more time."

"Go home and take a hot bath. I'll come by and give you a rub tomorrow, fix you something good to eat. Nothing heavy. I don't want you eating anything heavy." Bonnie patted Sara on the knee. Sara twisted and kinked the end of the terry cloth belt, unkinked it and twisted it again.

"Let me do the worrying," Bonnie said, wishing she could give Sara a good, long hug. She lit a cigarette and sucked it hard. "Go home and get some sleep," Bon advised, gently fingering Sara's hair.

"You go ahead, I want to sit here a little while longer."

"All right, but no brooding," Bon replied, reluctantly pulling away. She put her jacket on, zipped it up, patted Sara's head one more time and said goodnight.

"Night, BonBon."

Sara watched the older woman leave, then leaned back in her chair and closed her eyes. The lights were bright and hot on her skin. She was used to it, along with the applause and the smell of response coming off her audience as she performed. What unnerved her was the fear her audience would turn on her, announce her for a nothing, a dancer with a wobbly step. Sara writhed awhile under the imagined ridicule.'

Tanya's voice was lost under the sudden, enforced whine of the wind. She kept her face bent to the page and repeated,

'Sara writhed awhile under the imagined ridicule. She squirmed and sweated, and her hand crept under her robe to stroke her roused clit, but then she felt guilty, imagining her downfall, and brought to mind the rave review in the Gay News instead. It had referred to her show as an "erotic coming out of soul, bestiality and love." Sara smiled, fondled each of her breasts before tucking them back inside her robe and knotting it tight about her waist. Rising, she moved center stage and practiced her belly moves. The best part was letting her belly go, fat and full; then she undulated and gyrated, shimmied into the rolling contractions that generally brought the house down. Strutting across the stage, she leapt and came down the hunter, moving in with her lust; poised above her prey, delicious twitches and spasmodic ripples delivering her ecstatic, Sara mimed the descent. It was good, she knew it was, yet her fear of the audience's wrath loomed again and filled her mind, making her shiver.

She imagined five uncontrollably hot-blooded women shoving back their chairs, moving out of the audience up on stage, striding across the stage boards in their tight jeans and hard boots, undoing their flys. They wouldn't be able to take the tension, she on one side of the lights, they on another. They'd form a ring around her, and she wouldn't be able to stop them. After all, hadn't she enticed them? When they grabbed ahold of her, it meant she was theirs. The rest of the audience, roaring their approval, wanted her screaming; they wanted to see her insides.

Sara tried to resist the vision, but it drew her on. They were going to fuck her, that was for sure, with fists and fingers, lickerish eyes, and one of them had a dildo. She strapped it on while someone else aimed a few slaps. That brought another roar from the crowd.

"Shine those lights right up her cunt," someone yelled, and the one with the dildo climbed on top and went right in.

They wanted her to dance with that dildo inside, and when she refused, they slapped her again and again until she complied. They grinned victoriously amongst themselves, then one of them complained it was her turn to get on top. She did it with her fist and two fingers up the ass, mumbling something about filling up that big belly that moves so nice. She ordered the one with the dildo to shove it in the star's mouth, and for someone else to get a grip on those big boobies. They banged her while the audience cheered, and some of them were fucking, too, thereby proving Sara wasn't the only one who knew what was going on.

Each of the five women had to take a turn at her, then they threw her to the audience as so much used cunt. Of course everyone else wanted a piece of her, even if she was used and useless as a limp rag. "No more movement in her," someone sneered, and gave her one last kick as the lot of them filed out of the hall in search of a new star.

Sara wept for the vision gone, with fear that it might come true, as she went about turning out the lights save for one soft pink spot. She stood in it, arms upraised, uncomfortable of cunt; it clamored to be filled, but she had nothing to give it. "Tomorrow," she promised, opening her robe, her flesh beginning to prickle as she surrendered to a vision, her audience filling all the empty seats.'

Back at the writers' conference, Tanya closed her notebook, picked up the glass of water at her feet and drank it. She stood up, clutching her stories, and the audience stood with her, uncertain, with jangled nerves and labia. They didn't know whether to applaud or demand more; protest, or look around for someone to couple with. Luckily, Leigh broke the tension. She stretched to the tips of her toes at the back of the room and announced the reception in the adjoining room. The crowd started to mill and chat, gathering in little clumps to discuss what they'd just heard. Now that it was over, Tanya was flushed and slightly drained, though calm. Outside the wind raged.

In the other room a long table was clothed in white. There was champagne on ice in a small tin wash tub; paté and bread, bowls of relishes, cookies; enough to serve the hundred or so women present. Leigh chatted with several women she knew, all the while keeping an eye on Chanel who'd agreed to approach the tall woman Leigh had noticed earlier and wanted to meet. Leigh wiped dust off a potted plant as she kept track of Chanel with peripheral vision. Chanel's laughter bounced across the room as she helped Mary find more cups in the boxes under the table. Then she rearranged the centerpiece flowers, smelled them, caught Leigh's eye across the room and looked right on by, though she waggled her fingers in the air close to her hip, which meant Leigh should be patient. From there it was easy; Chanel chatted with this woman and that, slowly making her way to the far end of the table where the woman she was after expounded animatedly with two others. Just as Chanel approached, the two broke off to get themselves something to eat, and Chanel moved in.

Leigh watched Chanel make contact, laugh easily, offer the stranger a piece of bread and paté, then slowly drifted in their direction.

"Leigh!" Chanel called, waving her over, and when she was up close, drew her in and said, "This is Diana." Chanel bit into a round of french bread thickly spread with the soft oozy paté, then stood back a pace, cleaning up the corner of her mouth with her tongue.

"Pleased to meet you," Leigh said, registering Diana's green eyes, and the tiny silver labrys delicately chained around her neck.

Diana found Leigh's direct gaze and warm attention slightly overpowering. She drew herself up even taller, secretly noting Leigh's stocky strong build, and that her hands were blunt and sure.

Clearing her palate with champagne, Chanel asked, "What did you think of Tanya's reading?" Running the tip of her tongue along a celery groove, she looked first at Leigh, then at Diana.

Out in the night things rattled and bowed down to the storm. Leigh popped a radish into her mouth and bit down on the crisp fiery flesh. "The last story was unfinished," Diana insisted. She shook her head when Chanel offered her a carrot curl, then took hold of the tiny labrys around her neck and sawed it back and forth on its silver chain. "I thought Bonnie should come back. It'd make sense for her to go out of control, being around sexy Sara all the time and never getting any. Then Sara could have been ravished for real, not just in her imagination." Diana's lightly freckled cheeks reddened, she laughed and decided on a carrot curl, after all. Plucking it off the plate Chanel held out in front of her, Diana quickly glanced around the room as she munched it.

"But I think Bon really loved Sara," Leigh murmured.

"If she did, it was hopeless," Chanel replied, dipping an ice cube from the relish bowl and rattling it around in her hand before slipping it into her mouth and crunching it with her teeth.

"Still, if she were going to ravish Sara," Leigh continued, leaning forward from the waist to catch Diana's attention, "Sara would have had to accept Bon's love first, and Sara was into separating the two."

"Ravishment is ravishment," Diana declared, coloring a bit more, all too conscious of the sweat film beneath her clothes, the faint smell of musk biting her nose, and that Leigh's gaze had finished with her face, devoured her neck, and was now brushing back and forth across the slopes of her hidden breasts.

"The thing is," Chanel interjected as she examined the contours of a cherry tomato, "just how ready is the world for Lesbian Erotica?"

"Hey, we're full of forgotten and essential magical lore," Leigh said teasingly, and added, "they're ready," in the voice of a woman who's about to Top her willing Fem.

"You must write science fiction," Diana guessed, twirling the stem of her champagne glass between two fingers, feeling idiotically, wonderfully giddy.

Leigh leaned closer to Diana, conspiratorially, her fingertips lightly singeing Diana's skin, and in a lowered voice, quoted, "The Soul Patrol came over a ridge of desert land at midnight; marking the circle of purification, they ran at each other in mock battle, lunging and feinting and slashing under a full moon, the moon of Beltane."

Chanel drew the insides of the cherry tomato into her mouth as she watched Diana loosen with new fascination; watched Leigh reel her in in that inimitable way she had of getting to know someone; immersing herself in each and every sight, sound and word. Chanel knew it well, had seen it happen time and again, ever since she and Leigh had stopped being lovers long ago. Chanel held aloft a bottle and indicated she'd like to pour another round. Leigh leaned against Chanel's warm and substantial weight until her wine glass was full, silently thanked Chanel with a look at once tender and smirky, then reached across Chanel's front for a cherry tomato of her own. She rolled it around and around in her hollowed palm, studied its deep red skin, its lolling excellence and the crisp green top knot.

"The tomato lay calmly in the palm, waiting to be eaten," Leigh said, and with simple ceremony, offered it to Diana who took it and bit it, quickly cupping a hand beneath her chin to catch the seed spurting from between her lips.

"Hmmm!" she exclaimed, giggling and slurping; her pleasure turned to dismay, however, when some of the seeds did escape and stained her blouse. She was embarrassed by Leigh's rescue with a napkin Chanel dipped in some water, and insisting, "It's fine, I'll just go up to my room and change into something else," she made as if to leave.

"I know how to get stains out," Leigh insisted. "I'm coming with you to make sure it's done right."

Diana's protestations died in her throat when she realized how hard her nipples were in response to the gentle dabbling Leigh had done on her front. Feeling the situation was blatantly obvious, though, Diana smiled nervously at Chanel; finding no opposition there, Diana, vain, glorious now, carelessly unconcerned about her blouse because soon it would be stripped from her, hoped Leigh could smell the secret damp odor from between her legs.

"Take some food with you," Chanel said, extending a paper plate loaded down with bread slices, celery dipped in paté, and cookies.

"No cherry tomatoes?" Leigh joked, squeezing Chanel's shoulder, then briefly massaging her neck before letting her hand fall away. She turned to Diana and indicated she should lead the way. Diana said goodbye, and self conscious, made her exit into the hall. They waited for the elevator, Diana making note of the decor, Leigh rocking back and forth from heel to ball, unabashedly absorbing the faintly stout proportions of Diana's hips. The elevator walls were richly carpeted, their ascent quiet, then the door swished open, and the muffled report of their shoes along the corridor brought them to Diana's door. The room was mauve and gray, the rug creamy shag, and the queen sized bed was indented where Diana had laid on it earlier to test the mattress. The view was the wild lake and the dark matted swirl of surrounding trees. Placing the plate of food on the coffee table, Leigh went directly to the window. Diana stepped out of her low pumps and went into the bathroom where water was heard, splashing in the basin.

"I have Dom Perignon," Diana announced, returning with cleansed face and freshly brushed hair. She opened the tiny ice box the hotel provided, and holding up a jade bottle with a simple gold label, she slit the silver foil at the neck with her fingernail. Using the hem of her blouse to keep the cork from shooting across the room, she twisted it free, with a satisfying, forceful pop. She even had her own crystal ware which she carefully removed from a brown suede bag.

"Here's to writers, hmm?" she said, handing Leigh one of the long stemmed flutes. Their toast rang melodious in the air.

"My, my, my!" Leigh said, her eyes widening as the rare liquid went down.

"It was a birthday gift." Diana crossed the room, her nerves, fibers and veins pulsating with readiness; angling her hip and shoulder out from the windowsill while pressing her other leg against its firm base, she stood next to Leigh, opened up for her advance.

"We forgot your blouse! Take it off," Leigh said softly, setting her champagne down. Rain spattered smartly against the pane and the wind was whining again. Diana, her nipples aching almost beyond endurance, placed Leigh's hand on the top button.

"You do it," she replied, inching closer to Leigh who was momentarily mesmerized by the taut cloth over Diana's cunt, and the faint ridges of her underwear showing through her pants.

"You know the part I love best about women," Leigh said, searching Diana's face with a fervor Diana took for ruttish passion. "This part," She laid her free hand on Diana's haunch where the flesh had a tendency to bulge.

Diana flinched away, simultaneously tilting herself back into an even more inviting position: she wanted Leigh between her thighs. Leigh cupped both her haunches then, those hateful bulges just below the elastic lines of her underwear. A surge of pure hatred flared hot into Diana's heart. "Don't," she whispered angrily as Leigh persisted in fondling her there.

Leigh unhanded her and stepped back though she was still close. The building groaned under the beating it took, and the lake kicked and frothed beneath the cloud heavy sky. "The knife warrior cut circlets," Leigh said, her eyes steady and calm, her hands quivering at her sides, "one about each dancer's wrist, the other around the upper arm, then smeared ashes into the cuts so the blood went black. Thus, the dancers, a clan of shimmering bellies and legs, buttocks and breasts, were named."

"Your warriors are very elemental," Diana said sarcastically, punishing Leigh for not taking her right then and there. She shuddered under the caressing stealth of Leigh's hand sneaking back to those hateful bulges.

"Ritualistic blood, guts and sex," Leigh agreed lightly, smoothing Diana's hair back from her face.

"I want you to fuck me!" Diana cried out, despairing that Leigh didn't seem to know.

Leigh sighed, moved to the side and stared out at the storm lunging and lashing, bending the city to its will. "Can we get to know each other first?" she asked harshly.

Setting her jaw, Diana closed her arms over her stained breast. "By quoting strange excerpts at each other?"

The veins in Leigh's neck bulged twice their size. "My stories aren't strange," she sputtered, her face nakedly defensive, with hard orbs for eyes.

There was the heat Diana craved; the flashing knife glances, the balled fists poised and ready to strike, the aggressive thrust of Leigh's crotch. The very sight made Diana weaken. Her limbs tingled with renewed hope. "Yes," she hissed, "treat me like that. Do it to me!" Diana half hoped Leigh would spring at her and rip her clothes, but Leigh reached out and gently touched the stain on Diana's front.

"The ones kneeling did not move," Leigh whispered. "Even when the whip bearers danced into the center of the circle howling and screeching, cracking their implements and raising a dust."

"Touch me!" Diana implored, but started crying when Leigh stroked her flank.

"I could love you if you gave me a chance."

Diana tightened against the words. They were like fists slamming her in the gut, smacking her face, beating her to the ground. She sagged beneath their weight, into Leigh's arms, and panting, moaning, she begged, "Tell me again."

"When I saw you tonight, I wanted to know you."

The willing kindness in Leigh's tone tortured Diana to new heights. Terrified, writhing and squirming under the threat of love, Diana pleaded for mercy. "No more," she panted, and Leigh, sensing she truly was about done in, ceased for the night. The witchery of Beltane passed again.

NIGHTHAWK
by
Artemis OakGrove
$8.95

The latest from the dripping hot pen of Artemis OakGrove takes you to the underground world of the city ghetto where turf is controlled by fierce strength and cunning. Lori, unsuspecting, enters this world dominated by the warlord Nighthawk. Claimed, chained and branded by 'Hawk, Lori becomes the property of the subway Club.

Her struggle to maintain an identity, and 'Hawk's to keep control of her turf and her gangs, is interwoven with raw sex and sensitivity, dominance and dependency. It's another world out there—on Nighthawk's turf.

THE RAGING PEACE
Volume One of the Throne Trilogy
by
Artemis OakGrove
$7.95

Meet Ryan, millionare butch who flies her own plane, rides a motorcycle and wears leather. She meets and pursues Leslie, an attorney who has everything one wants in a femme—beauty, brains and passion. The surrounding cast of bitchy femmes, dominating dykes, sex slaves and naive high school girls are all being manipulated by the deadly Anara—from another world 3000 years past.

DREAMS OF VENGEANCE
Volume Two of the Throne Trilogy
by
Artemis OakGrove
$7.95

Continuing the sage of the luxury of a shared life—Ryan and Leslie, attended by their sex slaves Sanji and Corelle—a life filled with excesses from sex to sumptious living. But in the background lurks the demi-goddess Anara, bent on revenge against the members of her clan who where responsible for her death 3000 years before.

THRONE OF COUNCIL
Volume Three of the Throne Trilogy
by
Artemis OakGrove
$7.95

The spell-binding conclusion of the Throne Trilogy. Anara plans to deliver the final blow to Ryan, her only contender for the coveted role of Queen Regent of the Throne of Council. But even she doesn't know the true identity of the reigning Queen Regent who is determined to stop her and pass the succession on to Ryan who would rule the spirit world with love and compassion for milleniums – or until another such as Anara lusts for power and dominance . . .

TRAVELS WITH DIANA HUNTER
by
Regine Sands
$8.95

"From the first innocent nuzzle at the 'neck of nirvana' to the final orgasmic fulfillment, Regine Sands stirs us with her verbal foreplay, tongue in cheek humor and tongue in many other places eroticism."
— Jewelle Gomez

When sixteen-year-old Diana Hunter and Christine Tyler run away from Lubbock, Texas together it is the beginning of an odyssey that spans almost two decades of togetherness and separation. And in that separation, Diana must deal with a veritable parade of women attracted by her brilliance, her wit, but most of all – her body.

JOURNEY TO ZELINDAR
by
Diana Rivers
$9.95

Lace's first Lesbian adventure fantasy " . . . follows Sair as she flees the male enclave of Eezore and crosses the Red Line which marks the boundary of the Hadra dominions. What she discovers is a society of adventurous women, where Lesbianism is the norm and psychic rather than physical weapons are used in war. Rivers has done an incredible job in creating her world, which unfolds before us in all of its wonders and with a wealth of detail."
— *The Weekly News*

A THIRD STORY
by
Carole Taylor
$7.95

At a time when many gays would retreat to the closet and lock the door behind them, here is a novel that tells how women from three generations deal with coming out in a college community. When one woman decides to fight the battle of salary equity, a threat of exposure is used to silence her. With her lover, a lawyer, she decides to fight back in court. Her action touches students and staff members as they deal with the color lavender.

Ms. Taylor tells the tale with all the wit and wisdom of *Up the Down Staircase.* You'll find someone you know—or would like to—on every page. And, Ms. Taylor is donating 10% of her profits to AIDS research and to benefit AIDS patients.

JUST HOLD ME
by
Linda Parks
$7.95

Why has Constance Brooks been sentenced to prison for a crime she did not commit? Her lover's mother, the residents and the criminal justice system of a small midwest community don't really care. She isn't the kind of woman they understand or even want to try. From prison, Constance tries to prove she did not kill her lover. Discover how the American justice system works—or doesn't work—and how women forced to live subject to it find ways to cope and survive.

ORDER TODAY (clip or photocopy this coupon)

_____ copies	The Raging Peace	00–1	$7.95 ea. = _____
_____ copies	Dreams of Vengeance	05–2	$7.95 ea. = _____
_____ copies	Throne of Council	08–7	$7.95 ea. = _____
_____ copies	A Third Story	06–0	$7.95 ea. = _____
_____ copies	Travels with Diana Hunter	07–9	$8.95 ea. = _____
_____ copies	Just Hold Me	02–8	$7.95 ea. = _____
_____ copies	Journey to Zelindar	10–9	$9.95 ea. = _____
_____ copies	Nighthawk	11–7	$8.95 ea. = _____
_____ copies	Daughters of Khaton	03–6	$7.95 ea. = _____

Colorado residents please add 3.6% tax = _____

Postage/handling in US & Canada $1.50 = 1.50

Total in US funds = _____

_____ enclosed check or money order

_____ charge my MasterCard/VISA   account # _____

expiration date _____   signature _____

Name _____

Address _____

City _____ State _____ Zip _____

Send order form and payment to: Lace Publications, PO Box 10037, Denver, CO 80210–0037 USA

THANK YOU.